HOME
OF
THE HEART

•

LINDA MOORE

AVALON BOOKS
THOMAS BOUREGY AND COMPANY, INC.
401 LAFAYETTE STREET
NEW YORK, NEW YORK 10003

PRINTED IN THE UNITED STATES OF AMERICA
ON ACID-FREE PAPER
BY HADDON CRAFTSMEN, SCRANTON, PENNSYLVANIA

F
MOO

Moore, Linda
    Home of the heart

HOME
OF
THE HEART

To all the members of my wonderful family, who have given me their love, support, and prayers always, and to my many friends, especially Katherine Sansom, Shelley Blumberg, and Arlene Rife, who believed in me and this project.

Chapter One

"Darn!*"*

Green eyes snapping with impatience, Meg checked the traffic in the side mirror of her little red Mercedes. The lane to the left of her was packed solid and she was trapped behind a delivery van traveling a stately five m.p.h.

Please, God! I've got to be back at the office in ten minutes or Roz will never get me to the plane on time. Meg's mouth formed a wry smile. *So this is what they call a "glamour" job.* Keeping one hand on the steering wheel, she flipped her thick red hair out of the way and methodically began to massage her aching back and neck. The muscles under her fingers were tight as a drum. No wonder her head felt as if it was going to wrench from her neck and go shooting into space.

Meg switched off the car radio. Even the normally mellow sounds of New Age music on The Wave had an anxious quality; probably an overdose of Excedrin made it

1

seem so. Her colleagues at Frederick and Morrison Interiors, where she had worked since graduating from design school four years ago, rarely saw her frazzled, even though she worked like the devil. That's what it took to be successful in a town like L.A., and Meg had vowed to accept nothing less than success.

Phillip, the colleague Meg had dubbed their "camp counselor," had an uncanny knack for sensing his coworkers' moods. Just this morning he had rested his slender form on the edge of Meg's desk, blue eyes boring into her, and asked, "What's eating you?"

"Oh, you know . . . the usual. The fabric I back-ordered in September for the Meyers job has finally been traced to a barge stuck in an ice floe somewhere on the Great Lakes. I know Mrs. Meyers thought I was lying when I called her this morning to tell her. She's hopping mad because there's no way I can get that couch finished in time for her big New Year's Eve party. It's too late to choose another fabric, something I suggested back in August and again in September. On top of that, the table I ordered for the Palmers was finally delivered this morning. I just got a call from Sherrie Palmer telling me there's a big gouge in the faux marble finish, and how are they 'ever going to have Christmas dinner with it looking like that?' I've got to get over there and take a look at it at one o'clock this afternoon before my flight leaves." Meg gave a mighty sigh. "You know, I think I'll just skip Christmas this year."

"Meg, I'm surprised at you!"

"What do you mean?" The last thing she needed was Phillip to dish it to her.

"I've seen you handle twice as many crises in one morning without so much as a ruffled feather. Come on, you can tell old Phil. What's the real problem? Has it got something to do with your trip? You're going home, aren't you?''

''Phillip, have you thought about getting into counseling? You could bill yourself as *The Designers' Therapist*—sort of like, *Hairdresser to the Stars*.''

Phillip ran his fingers through his spiked, bleached-blond hair. ''You're avoiding the question. Fess up!'' He glowered at her menacingly.

''Doctor!'' she giggled, ''You'll lose more patients than you cure if you insist on such methods of interrogation.''

Phillip continued his glare, refusing to be thrown off the subject.

''It's really nothing. It's just that whenever I go home, my mother wants to know how often I go to church, why I'm not married and don't have a dozen children. And my father . . .'' Meg's voice rose. ''My father acts as if I'm still his little girl. Each time I see him, he gives me his standard lecture on saving my money, controlling my temper, and finding the right man to take care of me!''

Amusement danced in Phillip's eyes. Using his best Freudian accent, he leaned back and folded his hands across his chest. ''Ah, the old, 'My parents don't understand me,' syndrome. Meg could have sworn the diamond in his left earlobe winked at her.

''So you think it's funny, do you?'' Suddenly, Meg's face took on a sly smile. ''I have a great idea. Why don't you come home with me? You can demonstrate the fine art of handling my folks in person.''

Phillip slid off the desk and backed away, holding his hands in front of him as a shield. ''Oh no you don't! This is your problem. You're a big girl. You can handle it.''

Yes, she'd have to handle it herself. But first she'd better concentrate on catching that plane, and it looked as if her prayers would be answered as the truck that had been delaying her progress turned off onto a side street. Meg pressed the accelerator and sped toward the office.

"Oh, Meg, I'm so glad you're here. We'd better run if you're going to make the plane," exclaimed Rosalind, greeting Meg as she flew into the office. Meg was constantly amazed at how her friend and coworker since day one at the firm could sound so cheerful, even in a crisis.

Meg dumped her briefcase on the desk, gave Phillip a quick good-bye, and followed her tiny blond friend out the door. With Rosalind at the wheel, they snaked their way through more traffic. "Are you sure you packed my present to your parents?" Rosalind was asking.

"Yes, I'm sure. I made a list and checked it twice. I can't thank you enough for taking care of the Palmer problem. Thank heavens it isn't as bad as I thought it might be."

"I've already called Joe. He promised to get to it first thing tomorrow. I'll let Mrs. Palmer know as soon as I get back to the office."

"And you'll take good care of my car?"

"Are you kidding? I'll handle it with kid gloves. I'm scared to death something might happen to it."

"I owe you."

"Hey, no problem. Zack and I aren't leaving for Mammoth until after Christmas anyway. Just be sure to give Pam and Alan a big hug for me. They're some of my all-time favorite people."

"Right," Meg said wearily. "You know, you could have come with me. They always love to see you."

"I can't be a buffer between you and your parents forever. Besides, I'm sure they'll have a full enough house with your brother and his family there too. Maybe I can come next spring. Tell them to let me know when the violets are in bloom—or the lilacs—or the rhododendron.''

''I don't know which you love more, my parents or Oregon!''

Rosalind shrugged. ''How can you separate the two?''

''You don't. Anyway, I suspect you'd visit them any time of the year, except when you have a chance to be with Zack,'' Meg said, expertly changing the subject. ''You've been seeing each other quite a bit lately, haven't you? Is it getting serious?''

''Maybe.''

''That means you really don't know, or that you're afraid if you admit it, you'll jinx your chances with him. Well, I won't pry. I just hope you two have a really great time together.''

They arrived at LAX just in time for Meg to check her luggage, then sprint to the gate and onto the plane. She jammed her coat and hat into the already stuffed overhead bin and sank into her seat by the window, heart pounding. The plane was packed with holiday travelers heading north and home for Christmas, just four days away. Meg glanced out the window as they taxied to the runway. The mid-afternoon California sun filtered hazily through the low clouds. Although it was winter, she could feel its reflective rays penetrating the side of the plane, warming the interior.

After a while Meg became aware that they had been sitting on the edge of the runway for some time. The stillness of the cabin air and the press of humanity made her restless. Instinctively, she scrunched over closer to the window, trying to widen the space between herself and the rather large woman seated next to her. Meg noticed the woman's attention was focused on the in-flight magazine. The cover featured a skier soaring above white powder with blue sky behind him. Meg felt a prickle of envy for people who had the time for such carefree pursuits.

Time seemed to be elongating. Meg began to worry about missing her connecting flight in San Francisco.

"Ladies and gentlemen, we're sorry for the delay. Air traffic control has advised us that it'll be a few more minutes before they can clear us for takeoff. We know a lot of you folks are heading home for the holidays, and we promise to get you there before Christmas." As the pilot finished his monotonous speech, a groan spontaneously escaped from the passengers.

A few more minutes! It better not be long. Meg resented being at the mercy of an impersonal air traffic controller off in his tower somewhere. This was even worse than the entrapment she'd felt that afternoon in traffic. It was like the panic she always had to fight when she found herself on an elevator packed full of people—only worse.

The odor of dozens of bodies seemed to clog her nostrils; her sweater clung to her overheated flesh. She longed for some fresh air, but there was nothing she could do without causing a big scene. *If I tell the stewardess I need air, she'll think I'm nuts. That's all she needs is a fruitcake on her hands. Please, God, get this plane moving!*

The air seemed to have a tremendous weight to it, like a coffin lid. She hugged herself tightly and twisted uncomfortably in her seat. A fine mist of perspiration spread over her face. Her breathing became quick and shallow. With shaky movements she drew her knees up to her chest, assuming as much of a fetal position as her long legs would allow. *Another minute of this and I'm going to rip my clothes off and go running down the aisle. Either that or be sick to my stomach*—hardly a multiple-choice option.

* * *

Matt stretched his lean, jean-clad legs out into the aisle and tried to get comfortable. *Take a deep breath. Count to ten, let it out slowly. Again. That's good. Now, contract the back muscles. Release. Stomach muscles. Release. Good.* He pulled some papers out of his briefcase and began to study them. He'd always found this a good diversion. Today however, his eyes kept wanting to stray to the titian-haired, long-legged beauty sitting next to the window. He wasn't the kind to make a woman uncomfortable with his stare, but even in L.A., her kind of looks merited a double take. He'd first become aware of her as she hovered over him, searching for a place to store her coat in the bin above his seat. The delicious sight and scent of her shattered all his attempts to stay calm and relaxed for takeoff. Suddenly it was his heart that had taken off.

Matt gave up the pretense of reading and swiveled his head in Meg's direction and caught his breath in alarm. Huddled in her seat, her skin a sickly white and obviously hyperventilating, she was in trouble!

His adrenaline pumping, Matt swung into action. Grabbing the shoulders of the woman seated between them, he gently but firmly informed her that he was trading places with her. Before she had time to consider, she found herself plopped down in the aisle seat. At that same moment, Matt fished a white handkerchief out of his pocket and, with the most casual of postures, settled next to Meg. ''Hello, there,'' he said softly. ''Having a little difficulty?''

Meg continued hugging her legs, trying to focus on his words.

''I'm going to help you. Just do as I say and you'll be all right. Okay?'' His warm, steady voice slowly seeped into Meg's scrambled consciousness. She nodded.

''Good girl. Now, let go of your legs and place your feet on the floor. He gently pried her hands from her legs and pushed on the top of her knees. Meg stared unseeingly at him, eyes wide with panic. "Good. Now bend over a little. You're going to breathe into this handkerchief. Don't worry, it's clean." He gave a low chuckle. He held the handkerchief over her face like a mask. "Come on now. That'a girl. That's it. Take a deep breath. Let it out slowly, in slowly. That's good, Honey."

Meg's panic began to subside as she breathed into the handkerchief. The man's words were having an unintended effect on her. She was twenty-five years old and still people were calling her "Girl" and "Honey" and acting as if she didn't have a brain in her head. How dare this stranger treat her like an infant! Meg followed his instructions with a vengeance, taking several deep breaths until her head began to clear.

Matt watched the color slowly return to her pale cheeks. "Think you can hold the 'kerchief yourself?"

"Of course," she snapped.

His eyes widened at the sharp tone of her voice. "Okay, I'll just work on your shoulders a bit."

Strong, sure hands began kneading away the tension in her back. Feeling her muscles relaxing, Meg gave an unsteady sigh and surrendered.

"Sir, does the lady need some help?" A stewardess was leaning solicitously toward him.

"I think we just about have things under control, Ma'am. If you could find us a pillow and a glass of water, we'll be all set." Matt noticed that the woman he had unceremoniously dislodged was staring at Meg with morbid fascination. Matt patted her arm. "She's going to be just fine." The woman mutely nodded and returned to her magazine.

Soon the stewardess was back with the requested items. Meg did her best to hold the water glass steady as she drank. It was a struggle, as was her effort to squeeze back the tears of relief that threatened. She wasn't about to let this man see her cry. Gaining a measure of composure, Meg glanced over at him. His furrowed brow, the look in his deep golden-brown eyes, the serious mouth all reflected his intense concern. The aura of masculinity about him hit her with a jolt. Meg stiffened. This was a panic attack of a different sort.

"You all right?" Fleetingly, Matt's fingers brushed her cheek as he studied her face.

Meg shrank from his touch and dropped her gaze, her dark lashes standing out in relief against her pale skin. "Oh, I think I'll recover," she said, squaring her jaw.

"Believe me, you will," Matt promised in a husky voice. He cleared his throat, silently cursing the note of emotion he'd let creep into his words. That overprotectiveness his sisters frequently complained about could be a handicap sometimes. *Easy Matt, keep it light.*

"Five'll get you ten you didn't get much sleep last night," he teased.

"How would you know?" Resentment flared in Meg's green eyes.

"Just an educated guess." *Oooh-kay . . . I'll try something else.* "Now, let me make another guess. This time about your name." Matt rubbed his chin, seeming to be deep in thought. "Rose," he pronounced. "I'll bet your name is Rose."

Meg shook her head and turned to look out the window.

"No? Are you sure? You remind me of a long-stemmed red rose. I would have placed bets." He watched with satisfaction as the corner of Meg's mouth tilted up in amusement. He could tell she was having difficulty ignoring him. "How about Colleen? Katherine? Erin? Anna? Tara? Tracy? Uh, Shannon? Come on now, give me a hint. You don't deny you've got Irish blood, do you?"

Tilting her chin up, Meg gave him a defiant look. "Not for a minute."

"Well, then, you must have an Irish name." He gazed imploringly at her as she smiled smugly. "Kelly!"

Meg made a face.

"Uncle!" he exclaimed in frustration.

"Uncle? It certainly is not Uncle! Where did you come up with a name like that?" Meg stifled a giggle.

"I give up! You don't play fair!" Matt did his best to look hurt.

"Now, now, don't feel badly," Meg soothed. "I'll give you a hint. Mmm . . . it starts with *m* and ends with *g*."

"Let me see, now . . . Could it possibly be Meg?"

"How very clever you are!"

"Only one of my many talents."

Meg noticed the sparkle of mischief in his eyes. "Meg . . . is that short for Meghan?"

"Margaret. After my *non*-Irish grandmother."

"Guess I'm not so clever after all. You'll just have to tell me your last name." He gave her a devastating grin.

Meg paused for a minute, considering the wisdom of letting this stranger get so personal. Suspecting it was merely his way of distracting her from having another attack and feeling an odd mixture of gratitude and injured pride, she gave in. "Carey. My name is Meg Carey."

"It's pleased I am to meet you, Meg Carey," he said in his best Irish brogue and gravely proffered his hand. "Matthew Aaberg at your service." He inclined his head in a little bow, surreptitiously watching her face for a reaction.

She accepted his hand, showing no sign of recognition. *Good.* It's not that he expected it, but people back home in Oregon did identify him from time to time, and the results could be awkward. Most likely she had never seen him before. She looked very "L.A." Maybe she'd never even been to Oregon. Matt continued holding her hand as these speculations ran through his head.

Meg wrenched her hand free. *Try to be civil, Meg.* "I believe you already have—been at my service, I mean. I want to thank you for your help. I've never been affected quite like that before. How did you know what to do?" Meg's words were clipped and coolly polite.

"I fly a fair amount. The subject interests me." Just then, the plane began to taxi and the opportunity of Meg's questioning him further slipped away. Closing her eyes, she gratefully tilted her head toward the stream of air whooshing out of the overhead nozzle. If she had been watching, she might have noticed Matt close his own eyes and deliberately control his breathing as the plane's speed accelerated.

As soon as they were airborne, Matt opened his eyes and glanced at Meg. "May I suggest your getting a little shuteye?" He settled the pillow on his shoulder nearest her and patted it invitingly.

Meg's eyes widened. Was he being seductive or paternalistic? It didn't really matter. Neither approach was going to work with her. The man might be oozing with charm and self-assurance, but she wasn't in need of a man—father or boyfriend—thank you very much. Meg had become adept at fending off this kind. Giving her sweetest smile, she merely said, "That's a great idea. Thanks." She removed the pillow from his shoulder, placed it against the window and settled down. *Score one for Meg.*

Matt had let down his guard to comfort the girl and look what it had gotten him! It was like trying to help a cat stuck in a tree. The creature might appear harmless, even beguiling, but if he didn't watch himself, he could be maimed for life. Figuring out a way to reach her was going to be an interesting challenge and he accepted it with relish.

First he made a mental inventory of Meg's clothing. Her black leather pants revealed a pair of fashionable boots beneath. The big-collared sweater, in a flattering shade of coral, looked as if it could be angora. An unusual gold and jade ring adorned her right hand. And though he noticed the short, manicured nails, her left hand was tucked under her head, so he had to guess that she wasn't wearing a wedding ring. The scent of her perfume was exotic, sensual, and no doubt expensive. She was some kind of professional, most likely successful, probably single—mid twenties.

From where Matt was sitting, he could see her profile against the pillow: a strong face, full eyebrows, a good nose that was pleasantly rounded on the end, a generous mouth, a creamy complexion, tantalizing green eyes (though closed now), and *great* hair. Except for the hair and eyes, her individual features were nothing special, but the total effect was stunning.

Her temper was in evidence, but so were the humor and vulnerability. He wondered what she was like under normal circumstances. What might it be like to stroke her fair skin, the delicate eyelids, the slightly parted lips, now relaxed in sleep? His fingers itched to feel the texture of her hair.

Well, Matthew Aaberg, you must be off your stride. Here you are with a beautiful, fascinating woman, and you have no idea what's to be your next move. After conjuring up several scenarios and rejecting each one as ridiculous, he acknowledged the hand of fate, resigning himself to its further intervention and vowing to be ready for whatever opportunity might come his way.

Chapter Two

Someone was touching her gently on the shoulder and softly calling her name; someone who was warm and smelled deliciously male. Dreamily, Meg opened her eyes onto a man's face only a few inches from her nose. He had golden-brown eyes and was studying her thoughtfully. Meg lifted her head from the pillow with a jerk.

"I didn't mean to startle you," Matt said soothingly. "I thought you might be interested in the announcements, in case you're planning to catch a connecting flight."

"Oh, right. Thanks." Meg strained to make sense out of the voice coming over the intercom.

"Ladies and gentlemen, we are now making our final approach to San Francisco International Airport. Arrival time will be approximately six-thirty-five. Those of you making connecting flights should check with one of our gate agents standing by to assist you. We apologize for any inconvenience our late arrival may have caused."

Meg shook her head in disgust.

"I take it San Francisco is not your final destination?"

"No, I'm going to Portland, *if* I ever make it," she sighed.

"That makes two of us. I'll be glad to get back."

"You don't like L.A.?" Meg was clearly amused.

"Let's just say that a little goes a long way. Personally, I'd take Portland any day. How about you?"

"I couldn't disagree more. Portland is dark, wet, and stodgy. L.A. is bright, fun, and exciting. A person can be anything he wants to be in L.A. The opportunities are limitless."

Matt resisted the urge to debate. "So, you enjoy living in Los Angeles?"

"Yes, I do." She caught herself. How was it that he was so adept at drawing her into conversation? And why hadn't she noticed, until now, just how very attractive he was?

The plane began its descent toward the runway. Matt fell silent and they both turned their attention to the window. The blurred lights of San Francisco Bay became more distinct as they descended through the thin clouds. Meg felt a familiar thrill go up her spine. Landings always gave her a sense of new adventure.

Matt followed Meg as she pushed through the crowd to the gate attendant and stood where he could overhear her arranging her connection. "I'm sorry ma'am, but you've missed Flight 1178. It left ten minutes ago. The next flight to Portland is 2459 with the departure time of eight-fifty-five. There are a few seats left. Shall I reserve one for you?"

Matt knew his chances of getting a seat next to Meg were nil. If he didn't act now, he might lose her forever. Meg concluded her business and, as she turned to leave, Matt stepped in front of her. "Did I hear her say the next flight doesn't leave for two hours?" He tried to look disappointed. Fate was kind.

"That's right," she groaned. "It won't get into Portland until ten-forty tonight."

"Too bad. I guess we might as well relax while we're waiting. Care to join me for some chowder and some real San Francisco sourdough bread?"

Meg opened her mouth as if to protest. Matt quickly put his finger to her lips to shush her. "You owe me, you know." He prayed his ploy wouldn't backfire.

Meg was outraged. "What?"

Matt leaned over and spoke conspiratorially into her ear. "Come now, wasn't *I* the one who kept you from ripping off your clothes and running stark naked down the aisle of the plane a little while ago?"

Meg gasped and turned scarlet. "How . . . how did you know what I was thinking?"

Matt glanced at the people crowding around them. Several heads were turned in their direction. "Do you really want me to tell you right here, or would you rather wait until we have a little more privacy in the café?" The devil himself couldn't have looked more gleeful; he had her cornered. Meg desperately sought a way to salvage the situation.

"If I say *yes*, will you leave me alone on the flight to Portland?"

"You don't like my company?" He looked hurt.

"Let's just say that a little goes a long way." Meg tried her best to maintain her icy demeanor but the sparkle of triumph gleaming in her eyes was hard to hide.

Matt raised one eyebrow in reluctant admiration of her quick wit. "Are you sure that's what you want?"

"I'm always sure of what I want and what I *don't* want."

Meg knew she sounded spiteful, but the man seemed to bring out the worst in her.

"You've got yourself a deal, lady," he said grimly.

Meg felt a little better. She'd soon be free of him. "I believe I'm allowed one phone call and a trip to the rest room before I'm incarcerated?"

Matt frowned. He hadn't meant to corner her, only to get better acquainted. "I see the phones and the Ladies Room over there. Why don't you take care of those things while I get my reservation straightened out? Don't run off on me, okay?"

"I always honor my commitments." Frost shimmered on Meg's words. She tossed her head and marched toward a phone.

Sitting opposite Matt in the airport café, Meg studied the menu. Out of the corner of her eye, she saw him motion to the waitress who bustled over, asking, "And what can I get for you two this evening?"

Meg opened her mouth to order, but before she could speak, Matt answered. "Two bowls of clam chowder and a large basket of sourdough bread, please. Meg, what would you like to drink?"

Meg's eyes opened wide at his presumptuousness and her cheeks flushed with anger. Glaring at Matt, she replied, "If one of those bowls is for me, change it to just a cup; I'm not very hungry. And I'd like some coffee—black— with that, please."

If Matt noticed Meg's agitation, he gave no sign. Instead, he smiled at the waitress and said, "Just leave it at two bowls, and make that a large basket of bread, one coffee and two waters."

"Sure thing," replied the waitress, completely ignoring Meg. "I'll be back with your order in a jiffy."

Meg waited for the waitress to leave, then challenged him. "How dare you insist on ordering for me!"

The corners of Matt's mouth turned down in a self-deprecating smile. "I told you earlier that I thought you probably didn't have enough sleep last night. I also bet you didn't take time for lunch."

"Are you some sort of a mind reader? And how did you know what I was thinking of when I had that . . . that . . ."

"Panic attack? Don't be afraid to name it. I've found that the more you know about phobias, the better chance you have of overcoming them. I have an airplane phobia myself, so I've read quite a bit on the subject. Even went for some help. I'm a lot better now, but only because I chose to deal with it."

"You have a fear of flying? I never would have guessed. So my symptoms must have been pretty standard, including the part about the clothes?"

"Yes, it's a common thought, rarely carried out though, if that makes you feel any better. One of the tricks in dealing with flight phobia is figuring out the basic fear: heights, enclosed spaces, crowds. They say compulsive, high achievers have the worst time overcoming it."

Meg's green eyes flashed. "Are you including me in that category?"

"Well, you seemed in a hurry when you boarded the plane. You're dressed well—smell nice." He smiled mischievously. "I'd say you probably have a pretty demanding job."

"My job? Oh yes, it keeps me busy." For some reason she was finding it hard to concentrate. It seemed his smile was wreaking havoc with her brain waves.

"Want to tell me about it or are you going to make me guess?" He said it with such gentleness that Meg experienced a sudden meltdown in the region of her heart. After all, he had helped her through the crisis on the plane, and he seemed so genuine right now. Maybe she had misjudged him. "No, I won't make you guess. I'm an interior designer and, contrary to fiction, it can be a difficult profession. You're right, I didn't get much sleep last night. Today I ran around like crazy before I could catch the plane, and I guess I'm just a little tense about going home."

Matt detected the new warmth in her voice. "Your home is in Oregon? I thought you said you lived in L.A."

"Oh you know, *home*—family home, Mom and Dad, childhood, all that stuff." Meg wrinkled her nose.

"So, you grew up in Portland?"

"Nearby, in Hazel Creek."

"And you're not happy about your visit?" He sounded incredulous.

"Well, it's different once you're out on your own for a while. Didn't Thomas Wolfe say, 'You can't go home again'? But I'd really rather not talk about it."

"All right," Matt said easily. "Let's talk about good things. There must be something you're looking forward to doing this vacation."

Meg's eyes lit up. "Oh yes, I'm eager to see my niece again. She's six, and I haven't seen her for a couple of years. I've promised to take her ice-skating at Pioneer Square and to a performance of *The Nutcracker*. I got a letter from her the other day, and she sounded really excited about it."

The waitress brought the chowder and hot bread. The delicious aroma of the food rose on the steam. Hunger came upon her in an instant. She eagerly helped herself to the bread while waiting for her chowder to cool. Then, eyeing Matt with growing curiosity, she asked, "So, what do you do for a living?"

"I'm a reporter for a local TV station in Portland."

"I see you have a 'glamour' job too. I'll bet it's pretty stressful."

"It can be, but I really enjoy it. I wouldn't trade it for the world."

"Yes, I know what you mean. Sometimes I could throttle my clients, but then I'll get a project like designing a child's room, brainstorming about her needs and fantasies, conceiving the total environment and seeing it to completion. When that happens, it's not just a job; it's a joy. I can't imagine anything better." Meg's face glowed with pleasure as she shared her enthusiasm.

"Do you do a lot of children's rooms?"

"More all the time. L.A. is probably one of the few cities that has the potential for that specialty because of the number of upper-income families. I also have a job coming up soon in New York. The couple liked what I did for their son's room in California and they've asked me to do a playroom for him in their town house. It looks like next year could be really important for me."

"Congratulations." Matt tried to sound enthusiastic, but as she talked, he began to realize that their lives were leading in divergent directions. *Isn't that what you wanted to find out, Matt? Why take this any further?* Trouble was, the more they talked, the more fascinated he became. Perhaps fate was throwing him a curveball, but he wasn't about to let that stop him. Not yet.

"It's too bad that only rich kids get the benefit of your talent. I would think that less advantaged children might gain even more."

"Do you want me to change the world order? I'm afraid that's just the way things are. Even if I volunteered my services, there still has to be the resources to carry out my concepts. It's not that I haven't thought about it; I just don't know the answer. If you think of one, let me know."

"Gladly. Just tell me where to find you." He flashed her a triumphant grin.

Here it was. She realized she'd been dreading this question, and now she had inadvertently invited it. Still, she found herself unprepared. She glanced at her empty soup bowl, then slowly moved her chair back from the table. "Matthew, we're both very busy people—you said so yourself. I appreciate all you've done for me, but it's best to say good-bye now." She turned to leave.

He reached across the table, his large hand pressing down on her shoulder, directing her to sit back in the chair. "All right, if you say so. But first, let me give you a little advice about flying. Remember to concentrate on contracting and relaxing your muscles. Take ten deep breaths and exhale slowly. Say to yourself, 'I am going to get through this. I will be fine in a few minutes.' Here, I want to give you this to study." Matt drew from his briefcase a dog-eared book and handed it to Meg.

She read the title, *Fear Not to Fly*. "Oh, I couldn't. Don't you still use it?"

"I've got it memorized. Do as it says and you'll be fine." Meg noticed he was smiling that tender smile of his. They both rose. Matt extended his hand and gave hers a warm squeeze. "Take care, Meg Carey."

"Thank you." There seemed nothing more to say. Meg turned and numbly walked toward the gate.

Chapter Three

What a day! Ten hours ago, Meg had been going about her business in sunny Los Angeles. Now she was driving her rental car through a miserable, wet night on the last leg of her trip to Hazel Creek. So much had happened on the flight from L.A. to San Francisco. She'd been frightened, grateful, angry, captivated, and sad, all with an intensity that left her reeling. Meg tried to sort it out between San Francisco and Portland. She was reminded of the puzzle box she'd played with as a child. After some trial and error, she learned to fit differently shaped objects into their matching holes in the lid of the box. What she needed now was something like that box, a place to neatly file away her conflicting emotions.

The panic attack had been disturbing; she couldn't deny it. She'd read Matt's book and figured out why it had happened and what she could do about it. She was certain she could find a solution to that—that was the easy part. More

21

complex were two other pieces of the puzzle: a man named
Matthew Aaberg, and her response to him. Matt was a grab
bag of contradictions: *self-assured, chauvinistic, tender,*
and, oh yes! *terribly attractive!* But what did it matter who
he was or how he made her feel? He had gone out of her
life as quickly as he had entered it. She would never see
him again; she had made certain of that. Still, she looked
for him after deplaning in Portland, but he had vanished.
All she had left of him was a small book tucked carefully
away in her bag, and the feeling of loss that washed over
her. She told herself that the whole thing was probably just
a product of her overwrought imagination. Best to let it go
and concentrate on what lay directly ahead of her.

The windshield wipers of her rental car continued to beat
a gloomy cadence. Going home for Christmas wasn't exactly Meg's idea of fun. The sinking feeling in the pit of
her stomach returned each time she recalled her mother's
letter.

Dear Meg,

*I hope you haven't made any plans for Christmas yet,
because your father and I would really like you to come
home this year. You must see Kameron; he's such a happy
baby, and Eliza Jane is becoming quite a young lady. I
wish you could hear her talk about her "Aunt Meggie."
Besides, wouldn't it be nice to see the old home again? You
never know how much longer we might be living here.
Make the effort, won't you please?*

We love you.

Mother

Mom had certainly been thorough. She'd pushed just
about every one of Meg's hot buttons—those labeled

"guilt" and "obligation." At least Meg knew what to expect from her family. They were nothing if not consistent.

Meg turned onto the familiar street and drove slowly toward the old house. Before her mother had inherited it, most of the pastureland and nut groves had been sold off for a housing development. These days it stood in an oasis of trees, garden, lawn, and a remaining bit of pasture, its white, two-story structure rising above the surrounding low-slung ranch-style homes, witness to a more rural past.

It was almost midnight, but the windows glowed with light in anticipation of Meg's arrival. A string of multicolored Christmas bulbs framed the front door in a cheery welcome. Meg pulled into the drive and parked her car next to her father's pickup. Sighing, she clapped on her oversize hat, purchased with the Oregon weather in mind, and stepped out of the car and into the pouring rain. Before she could unload her luggage, her mother was hurrying towards her with outstretched arms. Father was close behind, trying to hold a large umbrella over his wife's bobbing head. "Hell of a night!" Meg heard him mumble.

"Welcome home, darling. You must be beat. Such a shame the flight was delayed. I'm so glad you called; we would have been worried to death. Alan, get Meggie's bags and let's get inside before we all drown." Mother gave Meg a damp hug. Together they gathered up the luggage and entered the warm house.

Meg sat by the crackling fire and Mother took her dripping coat and hat. "We won't keep you up long. I know you must be exhausted." She handed Meg a cup of hot cocoa. A melting marshmallow floated on the top. Father, after giving his daughter an awkward kiss, settled into his favorite lounger as Meg glanced around the familiar room. Except for her father's chair, the room had hardly changed since her childhood. The hodgepodge of furniture had been accumulating ever since her maternal grandparents first lived there so many years before. The Oriental rug was faded and showed much wear. The same books and china sat on their shelves behind the glass doors flanking the fireplace. The mantel clock still ticked steadily.

Meg's mother had pulled out all the stops in her holiday decorating. Swags of artificial greenery tied with big red bows were draped over every window and doorway. Christmas cards were taped to the door frames. Meg could smell the fragrant cedar fronds that covered the mantel. A wreath with an electric candle hung in the front window and a large fir tree sat in a corner, unadorned save for the familiar lights bubbling merrily. In short, the room was a decorator's nightmare.

Mother caught Meg's gaze. ''I saved the tree-decorating for Eliza Jane. I was sure when I brought her home with me from Salem the day before yesterday that she would want to do it right away, but she insisted that we wait for you. She wanted to stay up until you came, of course, but we finally managed to get her down. She's in the twin bed in your room. I'm sure she'll wake you bright and early tomorrow, so be prepared.''

''I guess I won't have long to wait. I'd better go to bed too.'' Meg got up and kissed both her parents, then climbed the stairs to her childhood bedroom.

Meg tiptoed into the room illuminated with only a night-light. She stood for a moment, gazing at the sleeping form of Eliza Jane and listening to her quiet breathing. Fumbling for her flannel nightie, Meg changed into it and climbed into bed. She had expected the sheets to be cold, maybe a bit damp, but they were toasty. Mother must have turned the electric blanket on for her. She settled into her favorite sleeping position and let the events of the day recede from consciousness.

*   *   *

From behind the door frame, Meg found herself peering into the living room. Her heart pounded wildly as she watched the stranger. The man carried a large cloth bag and was obviously looking for something. He paused, inspecting the objects behind the glass cupboard doors. Stealthily, he opened one of the doors and began to take out pieces of china, placing them in his bag. Knowing she was alone, Meg panicked.

"Protect my china, Meg," Mother had commanded as she left that afternoon. Her mother's admonition ringing in her ears, Meg ran forward and grabbed the fireplace poker. She raised it high above her head, then swung it with all her might, striking the man again and again.

Horror overcame her as she realized that she had killed the intruder! Filled with remorse, Meg moaned aloud.

"Aunt Meggie, wake up! Wake up!"

Meg fought her way to consciousness. Finally managing to open one eye, then the other, she stared at the small figure standing next to her bed. "Where . . . ?" Her voice trailed off. In a rush she realized where she was. She jerked herself to a seated position. The figure beside her took a frightened step backwards. "Eliza Jane? Is that you? Are you all right?" Meg asked groggily.

"Yes, Aunt Meggie," came the hesitant reply.

"What happened?"

"I heard you crying. Did you have a nightmare, Aunt Meggie?"

Meg shook her head to clear it. The dream was still vivid. "Yes, I guess I did. Did I frighten you? Come here, Sweetie." She patted the bed. Eliza Jane came forward and sat cross-legged next to Meg, snuggling in her arms. Meg laid her cheek on Eliza Jane's head and stroked the little girl's hair. "I'm awful sorry about scaring you," she murmured.

"I didn't know grown-ups had nightmares."

"Sometimes we do. I haven't had one in a long time. I must have had the electric blanket turned up too high. I think my brain got too hot!" They both giggled. "We'd better go back to sleep. We've got a big day ahead of us." Meg led her niece back to the other bed and tucked her in.

"Aunt Meggie?"

"Yes, Eliza Jane?"

"I'm glad you came home for Christmas."

"Me too."

Matt got up early the next day and walked across the plush carpet that felt so good under his bare feet. He liked coming home to his apartment after being away. The carpet, the beautiful hand-carved cherry dining set and a few other furnishings from his parents' estate gave him a sense of permanency. And his own black-and-white photos of some of Oregon's most beautiful wild places hanging in almost every room reminded him of who he was, what he did, and why.

Wandering over to his living-room window, Matt gazed at the rain and the view of the city that lay below him. His dark brown hair was a tousled mess, his pj's were crumpled, but his eyes held that dark, intense look they often did when he was concentrating on a good story.

As he studied the river and the other familiar landmarks of Portland, he reflected on his good fortune. His job with PBO couldn't be more perfect. At the age of thirty-one he was already producer and host of his own public television show. It gave him the opportunity to work in the city and still have the incredible experience of exploring the Oregon outdoors that he loved so well. Oh yes, he'd paid his dues.

Always there had been opportunities to move on and up, and he had seized them with a tenacity that never failed to impress management.

He was a lucky man, and today he would see to it that his luck continued. That enchanting redhead he'd met on the plane yesterday hadn't gotten rid of him yet, no matter what she might think. No one slipped away from Matt Aaberg that easily unless he allowed it, and he wasn't about to do that, at least not yet. He had to know how she'd feel in his arms and taste on his lips. His imagination was already working overtime. As he thought of Meg's laughing green eyes, the stubborn tilt of her chin, Matt's blood warmed to the challenge. *I wonder if six-year-olds take naps.*

Meg was first aware of someone's breath on her cheek. Then her sense of smell kicked in and she knew that Mother must be frying bacon in the kitchen. She opened her eyes slowly, not wanting to startle Eliza Jane who, Meg realized, must be standing quietly by her bed. The little girl stared intently at Meg, her eyes as green as her aunt's.

For a moment, the vision of another pair of eyes, thoughtful golden eyes, floated before Meg. She blinked the image away. It was too early to think about yesterday. "Well, good morning, Eliza Jane. How are you this fine morning?" Meg stretched and yawned.

"Very good, thank you."

Meg smiled at the formal way the child answered her. "You know, I'm feeling really lazy today. I think I'll just sleep a little longer." She closed her eyes, turned on her side, and let out a few dramatic snores.

"Aunt Meggie! Please don't go back to sleep! You promised we could go skating today, except I don't know how we can because it's still raining cats and dogs and I'm afraid the ice will melt and it will all be ruined.''

Meg laughed, rolled over again and hugged her niece. ''Don't you worry about that, you silly pickle wackle. The rink is under a great big tent. The ice won't get a drop of rain on it. Now, how about us getting up and eating some breakfast? I'm starved!'' Meg and Eliza Jane threw on their robes and slippers and clumped down the stairs, hand in hand.

''Good morning, ladies.'' Mother's cheerful voice seemed to mingle in the air with the tempting breakfast aromas. ''I hope you both slept well last night.''

''Grandma Carey, Aunt Meggie had a nightmare.''

''Is that why I heard you two jabbering away in the middle of the night? Was it about your job, Meg? I hope you're not working too hard.''

''No, Mother, it was nothing. I forgot to turn down the electric blanket and I just got a little overheated.''

''Oh, I'm sorry. That was my fault. I should have told you I'd turned it on before you went to bed.'' Mother's forehead wrinkled with concern.

''Please, Mom, don't worry about it. It's not important. Is that French toast and bacon you're making? It smells wonderful. I'll warm up the syrup. Has Dad gone to work already?''

''Yes, he left at seven-thirty. He and his crews are trying to finish up several roofs today so he can give his men the next week off. The rain of the last two days put a real crimp in their schedule, but it looks like it's slacking off now. Did you know there's talk of snow for tomorrow?''

''I can't believe it! You mean we might have a white Christmas?''

''Snow for Christmas! Snow for Christmas!'' Eliza Jane danced a little jig around the big kitchen. Meg joined hands and voice with her. "Snow for Christmas! Snow for Christmas!" Together they cavorted around the room, their slippered feet beating a soft tattoo on the worn floorboards. Breathless, they dropped into kitchen chairs, panting and laughing. Mother stood before them, hands on her hips, shaking her head in amusement, her eyes shining with happiness.

After breakfast, Meg laid plans for their excursion to Portland. "Are we really going to ride the bus, Aunt Meg? I can't wait. I've never been on a bus before!"

"Don't get so antsy, Pickle. Didn't you promise Grandma we'd decorate the tree?"

"Well yes, but what if we miss the bus?"

"The child has a point, Meg. Tree decorating is something you shouldn't rush. And besides, Sean and the rest of the family aren't arriving until tomorrow. Why don't you plan to do the tree right after supper tonight?"

"Are you sure you don't mind?"

"I'm sure. Now you two go get your combs and brushes so we can braid your hair."

"Mother, I've been braiding my hair myself since I went off to college."

"Meggie, you know I love to do it. You do Eliza Jane's and I'll do yours." Mother left no room for argument.

Three generations of Carey women sat single file, braiding hair. Meg carefully brushed Eliza Jane's dark, springy mane, gently working out the tangles, while Mother sat behind Meg, tending to her daughter's bright tresses. Meg understood why her mother had always liked this task. The work was soothing and created an unspoken bond between them. When they were finished, they all stood back and admired one another.

"My braid's longer than yours," singsonged Eliza Jane.

"The better to pull, my dear." Meg made a pass at Eliza

Jane's braid, but the girl dodged away just in time. "Okay, let's get dressed. If we catch the eleven-forty-five bus, we should reach the rink about a quarter to one. We can have lunch there and then we'll skate until our legs get as wobbly as Jell-O. Is that a plan?"

'You betcha!'' shouted Eliza Jane, parroting one of her grandfather's favorite expressions.

"Lord help me," Meg laughed.

Matt checked his watch again and resumed scanning the crowd. It had been a while since he'd done any real investigative reporting, but his instincts were still good . . . at least he hoped so. According to his calculations, Meg and her niece should be here just about now.

The rink was crowded with skaters of all shapes, sizes, and ages moving in chaotic patterns across the ice. Matt calculated that at any one time at least a quarter of them were either about to fall, in the process of falling, or struggling to recover from a fall. And almost drowning out the low rumble of the crowd were the excited shouts of children.

A flash of red hair caught Matt's eye, but almost immediately he knew it wasn't Meg's. The image of hers, a particular shade of mahogany, burned in his memory. He leaned his long frame against a post and relaxed a bit, a smile playing on his lips. Matt imagined a six-year-old version of Meg, red braids bouncing in excitement, as she waited impatiently for a promised treat.

Suddenly, his whole attention clicked to a movement several yards away. Matt caught his breath. He could barely see the back of her head through the crowd, and the hair was gathered in a single braid, not loose and swingy as before, but he was certain of who it was. His heart rejoiced. Matt caught up with them just as Meg and her niece were commandeering a rinkside table from a departing couple. Holding himself back, he let them get settled before approaching. Matt noticed with amusement that they looked very much like mother and daughter. Both wore turtlenecks and bright ski sweaters, dark stretch pants, and each had her hair pulled back in a thick French braid.

Taking a deep breath, Matt reviewed the scenario he'd mentally sketched. There was no margin for error. If he failed to impress Meg this time, he'd . . . he didn't even want to think about that possibility. Matt straightened himself and stepped forward.

"This is your man on the street, Homer Hicksville of station KNUT, with an up close and personal interview with two very lovely ladies who have, at this very moment, arrived at Pioneer Square. Miss, can you please tell the listening audience your name?" Matt shoved his imaginary microphone under Meg's chin.

Meg's heart stopped in mid beat as she looked up at the man towering over her. She could feel the goofy grin stretching across her face and she struggled to bring it under control. How had he found her? He looked wonderful. This time he was dressed in a business suit, but there was a certain outdoors aura about him that she had missed at the airport. Maybe it was the cowboy boots that extended below his well-pressed slacks—more likely, the light tan that made him stand out among the typically pasty-faced Portlanders. A warm glow seemed to emanate from him, beckoning her. Meg swallowed. "Matt . . ."

"You can call me Homer."

"Ah, yes, Homer. Perhaps you'd like to guess my name?" It was all Meg could do to keep from bursting into laughter, thinking about the first time they'd met.

"I can see that the lady has a sadistic sense of humor.

We'll just move on and find someone who's a little more cooperative.'' Matt half turned as if to leave.

''Wait!'' Meg jumped up and grabbed his hand, the one that still held the invisible microphone. They stood eyeing one another as she pulled his fist up to her face. She hadn't meant to call him back like that, but the thought of his leaving had sent her into a panic. The realization rocked her and she involuntarily squeezed his hand. It felt warm, masculine, and good. Matt quirked one eyebrow ever so slightly, waiting for Meg's next move.

''I'd be glad to give you my name,'' she said softly, ''and to introduce you to the young lady who is accompanying me today.'' She continued holding his hand as she gazed into his honey-warm eyes.

Reluctantly, Matt looked away, breaking off the spell. Another minute of having her close like this, and he'd be making a bigger fool of himself than he already was. ''Good, that's very good,'' he managed. ''Our listening audience is waiting with bated breath.''

''My name is Meg Carey, and I'd like to introduce my niece, Eliza Jane Carey.''

''Charmed, I'm sure.'' He gave Eliza Jane a low bow, then turned his attention back to Meg. ''Could you please tell our listening audience, Meg Carey, what brought you to Pioneer Square?''

''Well, as you mentioned, Homer, Eliza Jane and I have just arrived by coach to take in this marvelous, *marvelous*, affair at Pioneer Square. After a bit of lunch, we plan to don our skates and put on a dazzling display of grace and courage the world will long remember.''

''Fascinating! Thank you! Now, could we please have a word with Miss Eliza Jane Carey?'' Matt knelt down next to the girl and held the imaginary mike in front of her.

Eliza Jane looked at Meg inquiringly. Meg nodded her OK and winked.

"Tell me, Eliza Jane, are you looking forward to a fun-filled afternoon of skating?"

"You betcha!" she crowed into Matt's hand.

"Ah, *here's* a true Oregonian." Matt gave Meg a smug grin and straightened. "And now, for being such cooperative guests on our show today, let's see what prizes we have for you."

Meg eyed Matt suspiciously as he reached into the pocket of his sport jacket and brought out an invisible envelope and pretended to open it. Matt nodded in Eliza Jane's direction. "The young lady here wins . . ." he paused, scrunching up his face as if trying to make out the writing, "the Super Deluxe Burger Basket, including a large quantity of crispy fries, her choice of a soft drink or hot chocolate, and a hot fudge sundae! Mmmm! Mmmm! What have you got to say about that?"

"I say, *Let's eat!*" Eliza Jane shouted like a cheerleader, shooting her arms up into the air.

Matt laughed. "Now just a minute, we don't want to forget your Aunt Meg, do we?" He reached once again into his pocket and pulled out a second invisible envelope. "Ladies and gentlemen," he stage-whispered suspensefully, "what fantastic prize do we have for this beautiful young woman? Look at this! She's just won a full day of cross-country skiing on Mt. Hood with the famous tour guide, Matthew Aaberg! This fabulous package includes a delectable alfresco lunch and an even more tempting gourmet dinner, served fireside in one of Oregon's famous lodges, plus complimentary use of equipment *aaand* ski clothing. Let's hear it for our lucky winner!" Matt and Eliza Jane clapped enthusiastically.

Persistent and *clever* were two words Meg added to her

appraisal of Matthew Aaberg as she sought to squelch the rising bubble of happiness. She should be furious with him. She had made him promise to stay away, and yet somehow, he had found her. On top of that, he was trying to tempt her into making a date with him. It all sounded like such innocent fun, but Meg knew better. She couldn't go back to L.A. with her mind on Matthew. She had plans, dreams, and they were just beginning to be realized. She was beginning to make a name for herself as a sought-after designer in the rarefied world of Beverly Hills. This was a bad time in her life to get involved with someone, especially someone like Matt. Still, she didn't want to disappoint Eliza Jane.

"Eliza Jane, I suggest you collect your prize, but first you need to know that this character's real name is Matthew and that he's a friend of mine." Then turning to Matt, she said, "Would you take Eliza Jane and help her get her food? I'll hold the table until you get back. Then *I'll* get lunch for you and me. I'm in your debt and I intend to pay you." Meg watched as Matt and her niece walked hand in hand to the food counter, Matt's head bent low to catch what the little girl was telling him.

Meg hadn't said yes and she hadn't said no. Matt suspected she was buying time to think about his proposal. If she thought too long, he knew he wouldn't like her answer. He worried about it as he escorted Eliza Jane back to their table with her food.

Matt studied his two companions as they ate. Both had their heads bent over their meals. Eliza Jane was consuming her burger with gusto. Meg, on the other hand, was thoughtfully picking at hers, avoiding eye contact.

"So, what day would be best for you to go skiing?" Matt inquired with more bravado than he felt.

"Matt, I'm really sorry. It sounds wonderful, but my

schedule is awfully tight. I just don't have any time,'' Meg mumbled.

''I thought vacations were supposed to be relaxing. What day are you planning to leave Oregon?''

''The morning of the twenty-ninth.''

''And what will you do with yourself when you get back to L.A.? You can't tell me the design world is a hotbed of activity between Christmas and New Year's.''

''I just feel I need to get back.''

''Back to what? The rat race? Meg, when I first met you yesterday, you were really stressed out. Why not be good to yourself for a change, take an extra day? There's nothing like the mountain air and a little exercise to clear your mind and put things in a fresh perspective. And I promise, you won't have to do a thing but have fun.'' He flicked an imaginary cigar, wiggled his brows and leered at her. ''Trust me, Sweetheart.''

Meg glanced at her niece who was listening with rapt interest. ''Eliza Jane, are you finished eating? If you like, you may stand over there and watch the skaters.'' Eliza Jane bounded over to the rail and Meg turned her attention back to Matt.

''Trust you?'' she hissed. ''That's another thing. You promised to leave me alone, remember?''

''Ah, but that was for the flight to Portland. I kept my word. Besides, if I left you alone forever, look what you'd have missed.'' Matt spread his arms wide and grinned engagingly.

Meg gritted her teeth at the arrogance of the man. ''I hardly know you. I'd be crazy to agree to spend the day with someone I met once on an airplane.''

''What do you want, Woman? A letter of reference? After all, we've panicked together, eaten together, slept together . . . napping on the plane, I mean.'' Matt's face was a study in innocence. Meg opened her mouth to protest, but he rushed on. "And what about today? Doesn't that count for something?"

"I'll take the reference."

"Oh you will, will you!" Matt thought of the hundreds of television viewers who had just rated him as Oregon public television's most sincere personality in a statewide survey. Would it make any difference to Meg? And why? No. He wanted to stand on his own with her. His expressive face lit up with an idea. "Would someone on the staff of Timberline Lodge do? He can attest to both my sterling character *and* abilities as a guide."

"You don't give up, do you?"

"Not when something or someone is really important to me."

Matt scribbled a name and phone number on a napkin. "Just call the main desk at the Lodge and ask for Dave Olsen. He should be there any time after four P.M. Now, Ms. Carey, if you'll just give me your phone number, I'll let you two begin your skating. I'm sorry I can't stick around for your dazzling performance, but I've got to get back to the studio. I'll call you tonight."

"Make it after eight. We've got a tree to decorate." She smiled at Eliza Jane who was squirming impatiently at the rail. Meg wrote down her parents' phone number and handed it to Matt. He tucked it carefully into his wallet.

Eliza Jane headed for the skate rentals while Matt and Meg trailed after her. "How did you figure out I'd be here today?"

"Don't you know? At the café in the San Francisco Airport, I put you under my spell just long enough to implant a homing device next to your heart. I'm always going to be able to find you. Only if you want me to, of course."

Meg felt her heart give an extra thump. She almost believed him, and the thought nearly sent her reeling.

"I'll call you tonight."

Meg nodded, her head spinning with questions, warnings . . . and hallelujahs.

As Matt headed back to the studio, he had to keep his feet from doing a little jig right there on the sidewalk. Dave would come through for him. He was sure that Margaret Ann Carey—daughter of Pamela Stevens Carey and Alan Michael Carey, of Hazel Creek, Oregon, born twenty-five years ago last November 5 in Portland, Oregon, the enchanting redhead with the laughing green eyes—would say "yes." Out of habit, Matt glanced up at the gray sky and came to an abrupt halt. He stood transfixed as a peregrine falcon dipped its wing and sailed out of sight. Matt's mind automatically filed away another story idea, but his heart soared with the bird. He saluted in its direction.

Back in his office, he made a phone call. "Rachel, this is Matt. I've got a job for you."

"I suppose it's for yesterday?" was the tart reply. "Matt, my schedule is simply crazy, and I've got to get in some skiing. This will cost you."

"You're a real little capitalist, aren't you?"

"Darn right. I'm not in this business for my health."

"I want you to reserve the day of the twenty-ninth for me."

"That's Sunday! My fee is double."

"We'll see about that. I'll call you around nine tonight and we'll discuss details."

"You never cease to amaze me," the voice said, clearly exasperated.

"*You* never cease to amaze *me*, Honey."

Chapter Four

Eliza Jane was leaning drowsily against Meg. Following their afternoon antics, the hum of the big bus was making Meg sleepy too. Just as Meg had promised, their legs really had felt like "wobbly Jell-O" by the time they'd finally ended the skating.

"Aunt Meg, is he your boyfriend?" Eliza Jane asked dreamily.

"Is who my boyfriend?"

"You know . . . Matthew."

"No Pickle, he's just someone I know."

"Do you like him?"

Meg realized this was like answering the *Is Santa Claus real?* question. If only she knew herself. "Do you like him?"

'Yeah, I think he's silly!" Eliza Jane crinkled up her face.

"So you like silly guys?"

"Uh-huh . . . Aunt Meg?"

"Yes?" *Now what?*

"Are you ever going to get married?"

"Oh, I don't know. Do you think I should?" Meg guessed she knew the answer to that one.

"Sure. If you get married you can have kids."

Oh boy, Meg thought. *Eliza Jane is like all the Careys: direct and unswerving in her opinions.* "I've got you," Meg said.

"Yeah, but that's different. Don't you want your own kids?"

"I don't know; kids are a lot of trouble. Take you for example." Meg playfully punched her niece's arm.

Eliza Jane giggled. "I'm not a lot of trouble, but babies are."

"Like Kameron?"

"Yeah, but he's fun sometimes too. Mom says that pretty soon he'll be old enough to have a baby-sitter so she can go to school."

"Your mom is going to college?" Meg asked in surprise.

"Uh-huh." Eliza Jane let out a big sigh and closed her eyes.

Meg pondered this bit of information. For the past six years, her sister-in-law had been a model wife and mother. When Meg and Chrisy were high school friends, they had spent hours speculating about their future and planning how they would go to college together and become fabulously successful in their careers. But just before high school graduation, Chrisy had changed her mind. She and Sean, Meg's brother who was away at college, suddenly decided to get married. The families had tried to convince them to wait, but nothing would deter them. In the name of love, education took the backseat. Meg adored Sean and Chrisy, but she had never quite reconciled herself with their decisions.

Meg closed her eyes, wondering what lay ahead for Eliza Jane and her family.

Meg had called her mother from Portland, and she met them at the bus stop. "Did you girls have a good time?"

"Yeah!" Eliza Jane exclaimed. "I won a free lunch and Aunt Meggie won a ski trip."

"How did all this happen?"

"Oh, I ran into a friend of mine at the Square. He bought Eliza Jane lunch and invited me for a day of cross-country skiing," Meg explained.

"How nice for you, dear."

"I haven't said I would, yet. I'd have to change my reservation."

"Well, I hope you decide to go. It'll be good for you."

"We'll see." Meg wished her mother didn't have to get involved in everything.

Meg silently rehearsed her conversation with Dave Olsen, then dialed the number Matthew had written on the napkin. She felt awkward about making the call, but it seemed like the best way to learn more about the man whose image she couldn't seem to shake.

"Timberline Lodge," a voice answered. The words were a pleasure to Meg's ear. Mt. Hood's Timberline had been a favorite of hers since childhood. She supposed this was the famous lodge Matt had referred to in his wacky dinner invitation.

"May I please speak to Dave Olsen?"

"Dave Olsen? Oh, yes. Let me connect you."

"Dave here," came the booming voice. Meg could hear noises in the background.

"Hi. My name is Meg. Matthew Aaberg suggested I give you a call."

"Matt told you to call me?" He sounded interested.

"Yes. He said you could give me some information."

"Well sure, I'll try. What is it you need?"

"Matthew has proposed leading a little cross-country tour on Mt. Hood, and since I don't know him well, he suggested I check with you concerning his credentials." Meg did her best to sound businesslike.

"His credentials? Uh, I'm not quite sure why he'd want you to ask me, but I'll be glad to tell you what I know."

"Well, would you say he has the experience to be a good guide?" Meg's pencil was poised, ready to record his response.

"Oh, yeah, I'd say so. He knows Hood better than the inside of his TV studio, and that's saying something. Been skiing up here since he was a kid. No problems there."

"What about his character? Would you say he's . . . ah, reliable?"

"You mean trustworthy, honest, true-blue, the kind of guy I'd introduce to my sister?" Dave chuckled. "That's an affirmative, too."

"Would you mind telling me how you know Mr. Aaberg?"

"Mister Aaberg? As a matter of fact, Matt dated my sister in college. I was a couple of years younger, but he let me tag along sometimes. They finally broke up. Guess she couldn't take the competition, you know? Even then he had the girls swarming around him. He's something else." Dave halted, seeming to realize he'd said too much. "Anyway, we've remained friends ever since. I'd say you couldn't go wrong with a guy like Matt. Anything else you want to know?"

"I can't think of another thing. You've been most informative."

"You tell him 'Hi' for me, okay?"

"Yes, I'll do that. Thanks."

Meg set the receiver down and smiled at it as she reviewed Dave's chatty conversation. To hear Dave tell it, Matthew was some kind of a Boy Scout . . . with sex appeal. Well, it didn't appear that Matt was a mass murderer or a rapist. How dangerous could the man be? She'd go, have a fun day in the snow, and then head back to L.A., to her real life. Meg dialed the airline reservation desk.

It was suppertime and Mother had prepared a big dinner, as usual. Eliza Jane helped by setting the table in the dining room. Meg made the mashed potatoes. Meg's father came home tired but was happy that his crews had gotten their work done. They gathered around the familiar table which had not escaped Mother's decorating hand. The chandelier was draped with gold and silver rope and hung with gold ornaments. Sitting on the table was a carousel of angels propelled by candle flame, making a soft tinkling sound as they flew their stately circuit. Eliza Jane recited a short grace and they began to eat.

"Tell me, Meg," Father said between bites of roast beef, "how's life in La-La Land? Are you sharpening up on your volleyball game?"

Meg could feel the muscles in her neck snap to attention, and her temper began to simmer. "Yeah, Dad, I'm a killer at it."

"How's that little girlfriend of yours, Rosalind? Thought she might be coming home with you."

"Rosalind is twenty-seven years old, Dad. She's not exactly a little girl."

"Oh, you know what I mean. How's she been doing?"

"She said to send you and Mother her best. I think she probably would have come if hadn't been for Zack. She seems to be having a big romance with him."

"You tell her she's welcome to come any time," Mother offered.

"Say, what kind of car are you driving these days?" Her father resumed his interrogations.

"It's a small car," Meg answered offhandedly.

"What is it, a Beamer? They tell me all the yuppies in La-La Land drive Beamers."

"Alan, help yourself to some more potatoes and gravy," Mother interjected.

"Well, what kind of car *is* it?" Her father was as perceptive as a stone.

"It's not a BMW, Dad; it's a Mercedes-Benz 450 SL Coupe. I got it used—a real steal." Meg's voice was heavily edged with sarcasm, her temper now at medium-high. "If you like, I'll show you a picture of it. It's in my billfold, right where the pictures of my children ought to be."

Mother shot Meg a warning look.

"Whoa! I bet that set you back a pretty penny." Alan pointed his fork at her. "Take my advice, girl, and trade it in on something more practical. Put your money into a house or one of those condominiums, something that will be an investment."

Was her father ever going to think of her as an adult? She jumped up from the table so quickly it sent her chair careening, landing with a thud on the carpet. "What do you know about my life, Dad?" she shouted. "Did you know that I averaged twelve-hour days for the last four years to get where I am? I earned my money, and I'll be the one who decides how I spend it!"

The look on her father's face as she finished her tirade was like a slow-motion replay of a building being leveled by dynamite, his expression slowly crumbling into an ashen mask. Unable to bear it, Meg ran from the table and up to her room, hating herself for hurting him like that, hating him for pushing her into it. There had been similar scenes during her teen years, too many of them; but because she was now an adult, this was the worst. Not only had she hurt him, she'd confirmed his opinion about her temper. This was the very thing that she had feared would happen if she came home—what she had sought to avoid since leaving seven years ago. Phillip's words came back, mocking her. *You're a big girl. You can handle it.* Here, in her parents' house, she was reduced to childhood all over again. She was glad Rosalind hadn't come. Meg doubted that even her presence could have prevented this terrible confrontation.

There was a tentative rap on the door. "Meg?" It was her mother's voice. "Can I come in?"

"Yes, Mother," Meg answered with a sigh.

Pam entered and sat next to Meg on the bed. She put one arm gently around her daughter. "Eliza Jane's waiting for you to help her decorate the tree."

Meg looked at her mother, tears in her eyes. "How am I ever going to face Dad? I feel so awful."

"You could apologize."

"But I meant everything I said." Meg could feel the anger boiling up in her again.

"Maybe it was the way you said it."

"I just wish I could learn how to deal with him when he gets like that. I end up acting like a child, which is what he thinks I am anyway."

"Meg, I've stood by and watched you two go at it for years. You've got your horns locked. What you can't see is that neither of you is winning anything."

"I'm not going to let him control me!"

"I understand that, but try to see the humor in the situation."

Meg shook her head.

"Well," Pam sighed, "I hope you'll do your best to avoid another argument while you're here. Now come on downstairs and let's get that tree decorated."

Mother kept up a cheery show while Meg and Eliza Jane helped with the tree. She put a stack of Christmas albums on the old stereo, and oohed and aahed over nearly everything that was unearthed from the ornament box. "Oh look, Eliza Jane, this is an ornament your father made when he was just about your age. Can you find a place for it? Now where did I put the things you made the other day?"

For Eliza Jane's sake, Meg tried her best to join in the small talk. It was comforting to see the old, familiar decorations. She laughed when Mother reminded her about the year they'd tried putting shaving cream on the tree to simulate snow. What a disaster! But it had smelled good. When the last shiny ball and all the wooden horses and felt angels had been hung, Mother brought out candy canes and silver icicles for a final touch.

Meg made some hot cocoa and added a peppermint stick in each for a stirrer. She offered a mug to her father who was sitting in his lounger, his face obscured by the newspaper. Meg wondered if he understood that the cocoa was her peace offering.

The phone rang. Meg placed the mug on the table next to him and hurried to the kitchen to answer it.

"Carey residence."

"Hello, Meg? This is Matt Aaberg."

She felt like a teenager arranging a first date. She took a deep breath to steady herself. "Hi, there."

"Well, have you had your private investigator check me out? What's the word?"

"The word is, Dave Olsen says his sister should date you. Or was it that I should date Dave, or was it . . . ?"

"Whatta pal." Matt laughed. He liked the light-hearted way this conversation was going. "I should have known. Tell me about Meg Carey? Should she go out with me?"

Meg was silent for a moment. She didn't want to make this too easy. "Under one condition—promise to bring me home whenever I say."

"Sounds fair. May I make arrangements for dinner?"

"You've got to promise first."

"I, Matthew E. Aaberg, promise thee, Margaret Carey, to take thee home any time thee so desires."

"Then you've got yourself a date, Matthew Aaberg. Is Sunday okay?"

"Perfect." *Perfect!* "What say I pick you up about nine o'clock? I'll bring the ski clothes with me so we can go directly to the trail from your house."

"Can't I just meet you someplace? I've got a car."

"No, I'll pick you up. Besides, I'd like to meet your folks."

"You don't know what you're saying. I haven't had a date pick me up at home since high school, and with good reason."

"Why? Will your father ask me about my intentions and your mother measure me for my wedding tux?"

Meg laughed. "Either that, or they'll want to know why you're not taking me to church instead of skiing."

"Don't worry. I can handle them. Now let's see. You're about five-eight, am I right?"

"On the money."

"What's your shoe size?"

Meg hedged. "Somehow I never expected to have to give out that bit of information on a first date."

"Don't worry; I don't shock easily."

"It's a ten, narrow." Her tone defied him to make fun of her.

"Got it," Matt answered without a hint of a sneer. "Wear that turtleneck and sweater you had on today, and I'll bring everything else you need. Have you ever been skiing before?"

"I did a little downhill in high school."

"Good. That means the place I have in mind should be just right."

"Then I'll expect to see you the morning of the twenty-ninth. I've got to go now. Have a Merry Christmas."

"Merry Christmas to you too, Meg."

How he had managed to convince her to go, she wasn't sure, but she could add *persuasive . . . most persuasive* to her list.

"Well, it's all set. I'm going skiing on Sunday. I've changed my flight to the next day. Did Eliza Jane go up to bed?" Meg asked her mother.

"Yes, she was pretty tired."

"I am too. I think I'll take a soak in the tub and turn in early tonight. Good night, Mother."

"Good night, dear. Sweet dreams."

"Dad?" Meg tentatively approached her father's chair. "I just want to say good night."

"Good night," came his voice from behind the paper. Meg noticed that the cocoa mug was empty.

"Eliza Jane, are you still awake?"

"Yes, Aunt Meg."

"Did you feel pretty awful at dinner when I got mad at your grandpa?"

"Uh-huh." Eliza Jane stared at her braid as she twisted it tightly with her fingers.

Meg sat on the side of her bed. "I'm sorry, Sweetheart.

Sometimes I don't act very grown-up when I'm talking with your grandfather. It's something I'm going to have to work on. I just hope you and your daddy don't have fights like that.''

"I love my daddy."

"I know you do. I love my daddy too, and I know he loves me. It's just that sometimes we have a hard time showing it. Does that make any sense?"

"No." Eliza Jane looked up at Meg with wide, innocent eyes.

"I guess it doesn't make much sense to me either." Meg exhaled in frustration. "How about you and me getting a little shut-eye?"

"Thank you for taking me skating today, Aunt Meg. I had a great time."

"You're welcome. I had a good time too."

"Aunt Meg?"

"Yes?"

"If Matthew isn't your boyfriend, can he be mine when I grow up?"

Meg laughed. "I'll tell you what. Next time you see him, we'll ask. Okay?"

"Okay! Good night."

"Good night, Pickle." Meg kissed Eliza Jane's eyelids closed and tucked the covers around her chin.

Chapter Five

Christmas Eve morning Meg awoke early to a quiet house, its occupants enjoying a last-minute reprieve before the flurry of holiday activities promised to overtake them. The room was chilly, and Meg vacillated between enjoying her warm bed and braving the cold so she could have some private time over coffee. The need to be alone won out, and she steeled herself for the cold. Like a swimmer taking her first icy plunge, Meg tore back the covers and dove out of bed. Gliding across the floor, being careful to miss the creaky spots she knew so well, Meg scooped up her robe, scuffs, and Matthew's book, slipped out the door, and tiptoed down the stairs.

Reaching the haven of the kitchen, Meg peeked out the window, delighted to see a thin layer of white covering the ground. She studied the dimly lit sky, willing the tiny snowflakes into visibility. Maybe it really was going to be a white Christmas.

Meg plugged in the coffeepot and sat down at the kitchen table, letting the peacefulness of the early morning seep in. The coffee finished perking and Meg poured herself a cup. She sat down again and began to read Matthew's book. She was still reading when her mother came downstairs to start breakfast.

"Good morning, Meg. I thought I smelled fresh coffee."

Meg casually slipped the book in her robe pocket. "Yes, I got up a little early to read. Look out the window—it's snowing."

"So it is. I'm glad your father got the roofing projects done. I hope Sean and Chrisy won't have trouble driving up from Salem this afternoon. Did you get the paper?"

"No, I'll go do that now, then I'll make a fire."

"Maybe you'd better let your father make it. He'll be down shortly."

"Mother, I . . . Never mind. I'll get the paper." *Keep the peace, Meg. Keep the peace.*

Meg came back into the kitchen, shaking snow out of her hair. "Mother, the paper says that we're going to have about three inches of snow today and the temperature is going to drop to twelve degrees tonight."

"My goodness. I can't remember it being that cold at Christmastime since you were little. I'd better get my errands done early today. Would you and Eliza Jane like to help me deliver some cookies after breakfast?"

"Sure. I'll go dress and wake up Eliza Jane."

"Good-bye Pam, Meg, Eliza Jane. Thank you for bringing the cologne and the cookies. Now I'll have something to share with my friends here." Aunt Beth was propped up in bed, her voice frail, but her face aglow as she bade them farewell. Pam and Meg had squeezed her bony hand and kissed the loose skin on her sagging cheek. Eliza Jane shyly copied them. Together, the three Carey women walked down the steps of the nursing home, letting the snowflakes kiss their hair.

"That's the last stop. We'd better head on home before the roads get icy." Mother slid into the driver's seat.

"Gee, Grandma," Eliza Jane's voice was full of awe. "You sure know a lot of old people."

Mother laughed. "I guess when you live in one town as long as I have, you can't help but know a lot of old people. It helps to remind me of my own mortality."

"Come on Mother, don't talk like that," Meg protested.

"Oh I'm not ready to give up the ghost yet. I've got to see how my grandchildren turn out." She smiled at Eliza Jane.

"I'm going to be just like Aunt Meg when I grow up," Eliza Jane pronounced.

Meg laughed, but she couldn't help wondering if Mother was using the morning to give her daughter and granddaughter a lesson, attempting to bind them closer to family and its accompanying responsibilities.

"They're here! There're here!" Eliza Jane shouted. She'd spent the better part of the afternoon on the old overstuffed couch, her arms resting on its broad back, her nose pressed to the living room windowpane, watching it snow and waiting for her parents to arrive.

Once again, Mother ran out to greet her family, Father close behind to help with the luggage. Meg held Eliza Jane up to the kitchen window so she could watch. Chrisy, holding baby Kameron, entered the house first, and Eliza Jane made a beeline toward her mother.

Amid the talk, laughter, confusion, and hugs all around, Meg was introduced to the newest member of the family. The sleepy six-month-old promptly let out a howl. "I can see we're going to get along famously, Kameron!'' Meg exclaimed, and gave Chrisy another hug.

As soon as Sean and his family were settled in, Mother called them all to dinner. Meg was glad for the ensuing confusion: the passing of food, the talk, and the laughter. She and her father had managed to avoid each other all day. Now that Sean and Chrisy had arrived, their estrangement would not be so awkward.

''Meg,'' Chrisy said, as she deftly shoveled more food into Kameron's mouth, ''I ran into Toby Harris at the bank this morning. He asked about you and said to say 'Hi.' You know, he married Kim—the girl he started going with right after you broke up with him. They have two little boys and he's in data processing at Salem Bank.''

Meg involuntarily winced. It seemed that there was no part of her past she could avoid on this trip.

''Isn't that sweet, Meg? Toby was such a nice boy.'' Mother beamed.

Meg couldn't help laughing. ''Mother, I suspect you'd think Jack the Ripper was a nice boy if I was dating him.''

''He *seemed* nice.'' The color rose in Mother's cheeks and her eyes became very bright as she spoke.

Meg hastened to soften her words. ''I was just teasing, Mother. Toby seemed nice to me once, too.'' There was an awkward silence.

''Well, are we all going to the candlelight service tonight?'' Mother was back in command.

''Does that mean I get to stay up late?'' Eliza Jane's eyes were shining with excitement.

''Why would you want to do a thing like that, Pumpkin? Do you think you might see Santa Claus?'' Sean teased his daughter.

''You betcha!''

''Where did she get this 'you betcha' stuff?'' Sean stared

accusingly at his father, a smile twitching at the corner of his lips.

Alan merely shrugged and winked at Eliza Jane.

"Can I stay up and watch for Santa Claus?" the girl persisted.

"Tell you what—after church you have to go to bed . . ." Eliza Jane made a face. "But, you can listen for Santa, and when you hear his sleigh bells, you can get up again."

"Oh, boy! Thank you, Daddy." Eliza Jane bounced off of her chair and skipped over to her father who offered his cheek for a big kiss.

It had stopped snowing as Father drove his family to church. Christy had decided to stay home with Kameron, so there was just the five of them. It was not unlike the dozens of other Christmas Eves that Meg, Mother and Father, and Sean had spent together, except that tonight Eliza Jane was with them. Meg glanced over at her brother, wondering if he might be thinking the same thing.

The church windows spilled a warm light out onto the snowy landscape, beckoning to the outside world. The choir was singing "Oh Come All Ye Faithful" as the Careys filed inside. The scent of cedar and candle wax filled Meg with nostalgia. A giant tree stood near the front of the church, the star on top almost grazing the lofty ceiling, its shiny balls reflecting the light. Eliza Jane sat very still, snuggled between Meg and her father, taking it all in. It occurred to Meg that these sights, scents, and sounds were being indelibly imprinted on her niece, just as they had been on her.

The service was simple. Just before the last hymn, each person lit a candle and the lights were turned out. "Silent night, Holy night . . ." they sang in the flickering candlelight. For no reason she could identify, Meg found tears trickling down her cheeks.

They were all very quiet on the ride home. Eliza Jane leaned up against her father, struggling to keep her eyelids open. She seemed to revive when they reached home and she realized it was time to hang up the stockings. Mother helped Eliza Jane put out a glass of milk and a plate of cookies for Santa, then Alan spoke to his granddaughter. "Before you go to bed, Eliza Jane, I'd like to read a little story. Would you please help me?"

"Sure, Grandpa." Eliza Jane ran excitedly over to her grandfather who was seated in his lounger. Alan pulled the girl onto his lap and opened the book. Meg sat on the stool by the fire. Mother and Chrisy settled on the couch on either side of Sean, who put his arms around the two women as they prepared to listen. "It was the night before Christmas . . ." Alan began reading with measured cadence. "And all through the house . . ." Eliza Jane chimed in, her voice a high, chirping counterpoint to her grandfather's.

Meg let her mind drift to other Christmases—the ones she'd spent here in this house as a child, surrounded by family; the ones she'd spent away from home, trying to create her own traditions but always unable to capture the gaiety she thought she should feel; Christmases to come, wondering where she might be and with whom. She wondered what Matt was doing right now. Did he have a family? Close friends to celebrate with? She imagined him sitting next to her, his arm around her in the same loving and familiar way that Sean was holding Chrisy. Meg came back to partial reality as everyone joined in a hearty, "Merry Christmas to all and to all a good night!" The fantasy lingered tantalizingly around her like the warmth of a cozy blanket on a cold evening.

"Time for bed, Miss Eliza Jane." Chrisy drew her daughter from Alan's lap, escorted her around the room to say good night to everybody, then took her off to bed.

"I'll be to bed soon," Meg promised. As soon as Eliza Jane was settled, Chrisy and Sean, Meg, Mother, and Father took turns discreetly filling stockings and arranging packages under the tree.

Eliza Jane was lying on her back, staring at the ceiling as Meg entered the room and sat on the edge of the child's bed. "Are you listening for Santa, Eliza Jane?"

"Yes, but I'm worried that he won't know I'm here."

"Don't worry, Pickle—Santa knows those things. When I was your age, I slept in this very room and listened for him every Christmas Eve."

"Did you ever see him?" Eliza Jane propped herself up on her elbows, her voice high with excitement.

Meg smiled as she stroked the girl's hair. "Nope. I always went to sleep before he came."

"I'm going to see him. I'll stay awake forever if I have to."

"Will you wake me up when you hear him?" Meg asked, wishing it could be.

"I promise!" Eliza Jane's eyes widened with sincerity.

Meg pulled the string to the overhead light and slipped into bed. It wasn't long before she could hear the deep breathing that meant Eliza Jane was fast asleep.

"Wake up, Aunt Meg! It's Christmas!"

Meg opened her eyes. Being awakened every morning by an enthusiastic six-year-old was a definite change of pace. "Merry Christmas, Eliza Jane! Did Santa Claus come? Why didn't you wake me up?"

"I guess I fell asleep. I'm sorry." Eliza Jane seemed crestfallen.

"Hmm," Meg mused, chin in hand. "Do you suppose Santa puts a magic sleeping spell on each house as he makes his rounds?"

"I bet he does!" Eliza Jane said. Her eyes danced with renewed excitement.

"Well, let's not shilly-shally any longer. I want to find out what he brought us." Meg threw back her covers and got out of bed.

"Merry Christmas! Merry Christmas! Time to get up!" Meg and Eliza Jane called to the sleeping household as they headed for the living room. Kameron started to howl and Meg and Eliza Jane looked at each other, suppressing guilty smiles.

"He came! Santa Claus came!" Eliza Jane ran around the room, trying to examine everything at once. Meg plugged in the lights of the Christmas tree and surveyed the scene. It seemed that overnight the number of presents under the tree had doubled. The seven stockings hung by the fireplace were bulging, barely able to hold their contents. Eliza Jane stretched to free hers from its hook. "Can I open it now?" she begged Meg as she began to empty its contents.

"Not until everyone comes downstairs, Pickle. Go back upstairs and ask your folks to please get up. I'll put on the hot water."

Soon everyone was assembled before the fireplace, going through their stockings. Kameron, in his father's arms, rubbed his eyes with chubby fists, trying to fathom the source of excitement. Mother, in robe and slippers, immediately began taking pictures, catching everyone at their worst. Father sat in his chair like a king enjoying the escapades of his subjects. Christmas day at the Careys' had begun.

After a breakfast of sweet rolls, juice, and coffee, the family reassembled in the living room. "Is there anyone who would like to be Santa's helper and pass out the presents?" Mother asked as she looked around the room at her family.

Eliza Jane, who had been eyeing a large, brightly wrapped box, jumped up and waved her hand eagerly in the air. 'I'll do it! I'll do it!''

"All right, Eliza Jane. Who's going to get the first one?"

"Me! I get the first present!" Sean teased.

"Hey, how about me?" her grandfather pleaded.

"I think I should be first," Meg chimed in.

Eliza Jane stood by the tree, her hands on her hips, lips pursed in thought. "I know," she said, "since Kameron is the youngest and can't ask for himself, he gets the first one." Everyone laughed and clapped, including Kameron, and the opening of the presents began in earnest. Eliza Jane gave herself the second present, the big box that she had been admiring. Inside was a lovely doll, a gift from her parents. Alan unwrapped a brass log lighter that Rosalind had sent and promptly hung it by the fireplace.

Meg watched with satisfaction as the gifts she had brought for her family were opened. Mother was predictably thrilled with the lovely, soft afghan that Meg had knitted for her. "Oh, Meggie, you shouldn't have. When did you find the time?" she asked, beaming with pleasure. Father seemed happy with his Irish tweed hat. They all laughed as he tried it on; it looked so comical with his bathrobe and slippers. He protested when Mother took a picture, but continued to wear it throughout the morning.

Sean was enthusiastic over the racquetball racket Meg

and Chrisy had jointly given him. "Are you ready to take me on, Sis?" he challenged.

"You bet. I brought my racket hoping you'd want to. How about tomorrow morning at the club?"

Chrisy exclaimed over the cobalt blue candlesticks and vase that Meg had picked up for her at Conran's, and the bath powders, creams, gels, and lotions from Crabtree & Evelyn. Meg knew Chrisy didn't have much money to spend on frivolities and she enjoyed having the opportunity to pamper her a bit. "I can hardly wait to try these out, Meg. I love soaking in the big old bathtub in this house." Then Chrisy helped Kameron open his present, a complete Oshkosh ensemble, right down to the socks and sneakers.

Eliza Jane was the last to open Meg's gift, and she prayed that her niece would like it. Meg had thought about it a great deal, consulted with Chrisy, and had spent much care in its assembly. She held her breath as the young girl opened the box. "Oh, look. It's got other boxes inside," Eliza Jane declared. She carefully removed the four foil-wrapped boxes from the larger one. "Red, blue, green, and yellow." Eliza Jane lined the boxes up. "Aunt Meggie always gives me the most in-ter-es-ting presents. I wonder what could be inside." She held each box to her ear as she shook them. "Hmm. The only one that makes any noise is this one." She held up the yellow box in her hand. "Which one should I open first?" she asked Meg. Meg simply smiled and shrugged her shoulders.

"I'm going to open them all at the same time!" First she took off the ribbon from each box, then the paper, then the lids. Meg watched her carefully as the anticipation built.

Aware that all eyes were upon her, Eliza Jane announced in a dramatic voice, "Now I will look inside the first box." She folded back the tissue. "Buttons. That's what was making all that noise." She sifted her hands through the glittering assortment, then folded back the tissue on the second box. "Material." She glanced at her aunt, puzzled. "Ribbon and bee-you-ti-ful lace," she said as she pulled out the pieces of brightly colored trim from the third box. From the fourth and last box she pulled out a cloth bundle tied with ribbons. "What is it?" she wondered aloud as she undid the ribbons and unrolled it. "Scissors, thread, needles, a thimble, and some pins. It's for sewing!" She suddenly looked downcast.

"What's the matter?" Meg asked.

"I . . . I don't know how to sew."

"Not a problem, my dear, if you want to learn. I plan to teach you."

"Oh, yes, I do! Thank you, Aunt Meg!" Eliza Jane ran to give Meg a hug.

Meg returned it with a kiss and said solemnly to her, "Eliza Jane, will you promise to use these things very carefully and to put them away when you're through, so that Kameron won't hurt himself?"

Eliza Jane's eyes grew wide. "I promise, Aunt Meg. I know it's a big responsibility."

"Good girl!" Meg gave her another hug. "If you like, I'll give you your first lesson tomorrow. Maybe we can make something for your doll."

"That would be terrific!" Eliza Jane caught up her doll and twirled around the room.

"Meggie?" Mother was holding a package out to her. "This is for you, dear." Her quiet voice seemed to be holding some secret pleasure. Meg took the beautifully wrapped gift that Mother had obviously taken care in preparing. Filled with curiosity, Meg untied the ribbon, peeled away the paper and took off the lid. She folded back the tissue and gasped. "Mother, it's Grandma Carey's vase," she whispered with reverence, then glanced over at the cupboard next to the fireplace where it had been displayed as long as she could remember. Her dream came flooding back to her. The china, her mother's admonition, the man she had killed . . . and now the reality of Mother giving her this precious object.

"But Mother, it belongs to you and this house. I remember Grandma Carey telling me she had given it to you."

"And do you also remember her saying that someday I would be passing it along?" Mother smiled tenderly at her daughter.

"Well, yes. But that shouldn't happen until . . . for a long, long, time," Meg stammered.

"You mean, until I die? As I said yesterday, I'm not planning to do that just yet. But I want you to have it now, while I'm still around to see you have the use of it."

"Mother, I don't know what to say."

"If you enjoy it, that's enough. Just be sure you hand-carry it on the plane," Mother said briskly, obviously covering up emotions that were hovering just below the surface.

Meg put the vase carefully back into its box, then got up to hug her. "Thank you, Mom," she said softly as she gave her a squeeze.

Chapter Six

"That was a pretty fair game, Sis. Congratulations." Sean and Meg stood leaning against the wall of the racquetball court, trying to catch their breath.

"Pretty fair, my eye. It was brilliant! Admit it!" Meg playfully slapped her towel at her brother as they headed for the snack bar of the athletic club.

"You've been practicing," Sean accused.

"I don't deny it."

"Let's face it. You were a tiger out there, Meg. You've always been. No wonder Mom used to put you in the closet sometimes." Sean smiled and shook his head at the recollection.

"She did what?" Meg abruptly sat down in the nearest seat.

Sean chuckled, seating himself across from her. "Don't you remember, Meg? Whenever you had a fit of temper, Mom would make you sit in the closet."

"I'd forgotten all about it," Meg said in astonishment.

"I can remember you crying and screaming and Mom telling you to get into the closet until you were through with your tantrum."

Meg closed her eyes, trying to imagine herself as that fitful child. "Yes, it was the big coat closet in the hall. I remember sitting on a little stool, looking up at the overhead lightbulb and seeing the bottom of the coats. I haven't thought of that in years."

"I kind of admired you for standing up for yourself."

"Really?" Meg's eyebrows drew together. "I never guessed. It seemed that things came so easily for you, that you just floated happily downstream while I was swimming against the current. And Dad was always holding you up to me as an example. 'Sean this and Sean that.' "

"I can't believe you mean that. I know Dad is every bit as proud of you as he is of me. Maybe more so. How can you forget that it was *I* who disgraced the family when I got married before finishing college?"

"As a matter of fact, their praise for you only increased: what a 'darling' family you had, how hard you were working at your job and school, what a 'wonderful personality' you had, ad nauseam. I don't think Dad will ever forgive me for finishing college before you did."

Sean absently rubbed his nose, considering. "You always were a competitor. I stumbled and you took the lead. You finished your degree in three years instead of four, and now look where you are. As far as I'm concerned Meg, you've proven yourself, and I'm sure Dad thinks so too."

Meg snorted in disgust. "I doubt it."

"Why not ask him?"

"No! If he can't tell me on his own, I don't want to hear it!" Meg's voice quivered with anger.

"Suit yourself, but I don't think stubbornness is going

to win you this battle. Dad isn't perfect, but he loves us. Grant him that much, anyway.'' He caught one of her hands and gave her a little squeeze. Meg remained staring at the tabletop, unwilling to take up Sean's challenge.

Sean got up from his seat. ''Would you like something to drink?''

''Thanks, a diet soda will be fine.''

Sean returned a few minutes later with their drinks, seemingly deep in thought.

''Meg, I hope you don't give Mom a hard time about putting you in the closet. It happened a long time ago; I shouldn't have mentioned it. It's bad enough that you don't get along with Dad.''

''I don't know, Sean. No matter how hard I try to avoid conflict with Mother and Dad, it always manages to work its way to the surface. It's just easier if I stay away. If it weren't for Eliza Jane, you, and Chrisy, I probably wouldn't have come at all. I probably shouldn't have.''

''Family is important, Meg. Don't sell us short.''

Sean and Meg reached home in time to see Chrisy shepherding her children in from a romp in the snow. ''Daddy, Aunt Meg, Mommy says I can stay outside and play if you stay out with me. Will you take me sledding? Please?'' Eliza Jane danced around them excitedly.

Sean and Meg grinned at each other, recalling the many times they'd slid down the gentle incline of the road in front of their house on snowy days. Sean knelt in front of his daughter and said with great seriousness, ''If I were you, Eliza Jane, I'd make Evel Knievel here,'' he pointed to Meg, ''promise to keep her eyes open when she steers.'' Meg quickly made a snowball and lobbed it in Sean's direction. She supposed he was referring to the time she'd boasted that she could steer the sled with her eyes closed.

Meg had headed the two of them straight toward the telephone pole and a spectacular crash. The incident had immediately became a part of family legend.

With much whooping and laughter, Meg took Eliza Jane
down the hill a couple of times on the old sled that Sean
had uncovered in the garage. Then she begged off and volunteered to watch Kameron so that Chrisy could share in
the fun.

Immediately following lunch, Eliza Jane and Meg settled
down for the little girl's first sewing lesson. "Do you sew
at home, Aunt Meg?" Eliza Jane wanted to know.

"Not very much, Eliza Jane. I'm pretty busy these days,
but when I was in high school, I made a lot of my clothes.
I'm going to teach you just the way your great-grandmother
Carey taught me. Pick out a piece of material and we'll
start with a skirt for your doll. When we're finished, I want
you to take a nap so that you'll be able to enjoy *The Nutcracker* tonight. All of us Carey women are going, you
know. Won't that be fun?"

And it was fun. Eliza Jane was absolutely riveted
throughout the performance. As they left the theater, Meg
and Chrisy held her hands high so she could dance out of
the theater on her tiptoes. The four of them laughed and
talked companionably on the way home, and Meg found
herself enjoying their camaraderie. She tried to push away
the knowledge that Sean and his family would be going
home the next day, leaving her alone with her parents. She
wondered if she'd made a mistake in letting Matt talk her
into staying the extra day.

Matt paced back and forth across his office. It was three
days after Christmas, and he was hard at work trying to
decide between the vanishing salmon and the spotted owl
stories for his next show. He'd saved a number of features

from fall shoots so that his crew could stay in town for the holidays. The Oregon surfer item would be just the right "light" piece. His cameraman had gotten some great underwater shots, despite being slammed around by the heavy seas. Finding the best "message" piece was proving more difficult. These kinds of decisions usually came easily for Matt, and his agitation with himself grew moment by moment. Finally, he tossed the papers he had been pretending to study onto his desk, grabbed his coat, and strode out of the studio.

He walked quickly, past patches of dirty snow remaining along the curb. The sky was overcast with the promise of more snow. In a gap between buildings, he stopped and stared at a place on the horizon where he knew Mt. Hood was hiding behind a blanket of gray clouds. Like most Portlanders, he was used to the mountain being obscured during the winter months, and just knowing that it was there, hovering over the city, was a comfort. He stuffed his hands in the pockets of his overcoat, trying to quell his impatience, trying to tell himself that he was just edgy from being cooped up inside the studio for too many days, even though he knew it wasn't so.

He figured that just about now Rachel would be out shopping for the fresh ingredients that would make up tomorrow's repast. He had gone over the menu with her so thoroughly that she finally demanded to know exactly who this date of his was. "Come on, Matthew, when was the last time you paid this much attention to what I put together for you. And champagne! She must be really special."

Matthew looked worried. "Do you think champagne is too much? I suppose we could stick to the Chardonnay for the whole meal."

Rachel laid a reassuring hand on her brother's arm, trying to treat the matter as seriously as he seemed to think it was. "Believe me. Champagne is perfect. The whole thing will be perfect. Come over to my place the night before and I'll tutor you on how to serve it all. I'll have the lunch ready early Sunday morning."

"One more thing."

"Uh-oh. Why do I feel the other shoe is about to drop?"

"Meg's from out of town and doesn't have the right clothes or equipment. I told her I'd provide them." Matt looked at his sister hopefully.

"And I suppose she happens to be just about my size, and you're wondering, since I'm such a kind soul, if I could find it in my heart to lend her my things." Rachel stood with her feet slightly apart, her hands on her hips; the same stance he remembered his mother taking when he'd try to con her into supporting some whim of his. The memory was bittersweet, and he swallowed hard to clear the lump in his throat.

"You'll have to admit you'll be too busy that day to ski," he reasoned.

"All right! All right!" Rachel threw up her hands in exasperation, but the indulgent smile she wore told him her true feelings. Matthew gave her a bone-crunching hug in response, leaving her wondering about the effect this new woman seemed to be having on him.

Matthew had brought up the subject of the ski trip menu again on Christmas Day. He, Rachel, and their sister Sarah, and Sarah's new husband, Jim, were gathered at the family weekend cabin to celebrate the day. Since their parents' tragic accident and the eventual sale of the family home, the cabin had served as a beacon of love and family to the three Aaberg children. Even though almost seven years had passed, brother and sisters were acutely aware of the sense of loss that remained hovering over their gatherings. Jim's presence was another positive sign of the family healing itself.

"How are you coming with that catering project of mine?" Matthew asked Rachel when he found himself drying dishes with her after dinner.

"Haven't thought a thing about it since we last talked. It's Christmas, you know?"

Matthew suspected she was teasing him, but he ignored the thought. "Yes, I *have* noticed. I just want to be sure we haven't forgotten anything."

"What are you two talking about?" Sarah wanted to know as she brought in more dinner leftovers.

"Oh nothing," Matt said hastily.

"Matthew's gotten himself a big ski date for Sunday, and I'm catering."

Sarah raised one eyebrow at him as she munched on a stray piece of celery. "Somebody special? Do I know her?"

Matthew moaned as he patted the platter dry. "I should have my head examined for letting my family in on this. If Rachel wasn't the best darn caterer in town, I'd have kept it to myself."

Sarah leaned against one side of the door frame, laced her fingers together and rested them on top of her head. "Matthew, Matthew, Matthew. How quickly you forget the third degree you've given both Rachel and me about our dates. That's why I got married; it was out of self-defense."

"Why did you get married?" Jim came up behind Sarah and put his arms around her.

Sarah laughed, then turned and gave him a passionate kiss. "Because you're warm, handsome, charming, and because I absolutely can't resist you." Jim's face turned a bright pink, but he continued to embrace his bride.

"My, my, how we've strayed from the subject," Rachel mused, handing her sister the dish towel.

"Oh, sorry. What's her name, Matthew?"

"Meg Carey. And no, you don't know her."

"So, when do we get to meet her?"

"Probably never. She's just visiting the area for the holidays."

"You're just full of information, aren't you? Where does she live?"

"Los Angeles."

Sarah whistled. "Los Angeles? That's a long way for a date, isn't it?"

"Geez! Can't I have one innocent little date with the woman?" Matthew unplugged the stopper and watched the water drain out of the sink.

"I think what Sarah is trying to tell you, Matthew, is that maybe it's time you found *the* woman."

"You mean get married, settle down? Not likely!" Matthew expelled a short laugh. "I've got too much trouble looking after you two. Besides, I'm married to my job."

"That's a cop-out Matt, and you know it," Sarah complained.

Matt dried his hands and began rolling down his sleeves. "If you are so all-fired hot to marry me off, you should be glad that at least I have a date. And by the way, I've got this cabin reserved for Sunday. Rachel has promised to leave as soon as she's got everything set up. And Sarah, I don't want you to just 'happen' by."

Jim, who had been silently observing the three siblings, spoke up. "I'll see to that, Bro."

Matt's job was waiting for him, and he was glad he had it. Just now, though, it served more as a distraction than its usual all-consuming passion. He went back to his office, drew a coin from his pants pocket, flipped it, and settled on the subject of his next show.

Chapter Seven

Rachel and Matt stood back, studying the assemblage of picnic items arrayed on Rachel's kitchen counter. It was early Sunday morning and Rachel was on her second cup of coffee. "Have I forgotten anything?" she wondered aloud. "Soup, cups and spoons, sandwich pockets . . . keep them hot in this container until you're ready to hit the trail . . . carrot curls, Japanese oranges, cookies, trail mix . . ." Matt reached for a cookie and Rachel slapped his hand. "A little eager, aren't we?" she scolded.

"I just wanted to taste-test one to make sure you didn't put the raisins in this time." He was all little-boy innocence.

"Yes, I left them out, but I can hardly call them 'Kitchen Sink Cookies' without everything in them. Let's see, where was I?" Rachel returned to her list. "Beer, sparkling juices, cloth napkins, moist towelettes, salt and pepper packets, plates, litter bag. I think that's it."

"Good. I've got both pairs of skis and poles in my truck, and I went over the emergency items in my pack last night. Are these the clothes for Meg?"

"Yes, but how about boots? I didn't see that on your list."

"No, I had to rent those. That's where you two differ. I got them last night. Where's your pack?"

"Right here," Rachel said, beginning to fill it with the clothes. "What's the weather forecast?"

"It's still snowing lightly up there with a possibility of clearing a little later, which I hope it does. There's some spectacular scenery on the trail I've chosen."

"Well, it looks like you've thought of everything. I'll be up at the cabin about three this afternoon to get dinner set up. Now get out of here, so I can begin preparing the entrée."

Rachel helped Matt carry everything down to his four-wheel drive. "Matthew, there's something I want you to do for me," she said as he began loading things in the back.

"I'm at your mercy, sweet Sister." He slipped his arm around her and grinned.

"Have a great time. You deserve it." Rachel planted a kiss on his cheek and spun away, turning back to give him a wave. Feeling like a giddy teenager on his first date, Matt hopped into his truck and sped toward Hazel Creek.

"This must be your young man, Meg." Mother had been glancing out the kitchen window for the past half hour.

"Nine o'clock. Right on time," her father said approvingly.

Let this go smoothly, Meg prayed as she ran to the door. The bell rang and she took a deep breath before grasping the latch and pulling the door open.

Matt stood in the doorway, a sparkle of anticipation in

his eyes. He wore a wildly patterned Lycra suit and a black padded vest. The misgivings that had been building dissolved into happiness at his appearance. She had the crazy impulse to embrace him like an old friend, but she hung on to her composure. "Matt, hi. Please come in." Meg steered him through the hall and into the living room. "Mother, Dad, this is Matthew Aaberg. Matt, this is Pamela and Alan Carey." She gave him a sidelong glance to see if he was still as fearless about meeting them as he claimed.

Matt's face broke into a wide grin. "Mrs. Carey, I've been looking forward to meeting you." He extended his hand to her. "I hope I'm not interrupting your plans for church this morning. It just seemed like the only chance I'd have to spend some time with your daughter."

Meg was amused by the look of enchantment on her mother's face. She glanced at her father, who couldn't seem to keep his eyes off Matt's clothing. *Not bad, Matthew. Now let's see how you handle Dad.*

Apparently Matt had noticed her father's focus. "Pretty wild, isn't it, Sir?" Matt glanced down at himself. "One of my sisters gave me this suit as a Christmas gift. You know how women are: always trying to gussy up their menfolk. I hope, Mr. Carey," his face grew serious, 'that you don't mind me taking your daughter for the day. I figure she could use some mountain air and a chance to be reminded of what a great state this is. Don't you agree?"

"Why, yes, I suppose I do. We don't want her to forget she's got Oregon blood in her veins." Meg's father clapped Matt solidly on the back.

"More like rainwater! Have you got the clothes, Matt? I'll go change."

Matt handed her the bag he had been carrying, and Meg hurried off to her room, wondering which was worse: Matthew and her father at odds, or the two of them in league with one another.

"Might as well sit down. You never know how long a woman's going to take." Alan motioned to the sofa.

"Matthew, can I get you something to drink while you're waiting? Coffee? Tea? Juice?" Pam offered.

"No, thank you. I'm fine. You know, it's too bad Meg has to go back to L.A. so soon, but I gather she's got a lot of projects ahead of her." Once again, Matt was the crafty reporter, looking for a lead.

"Oh, my yes. Sometimes I worry that she's working too hard." Matt had touched on one of Pam's favorite subjects. "Have you seen anything she's designed, Matthew?"

"No, I'm sorry to say I haven't, but I gather that she is quite talented."

"You can bet she is!" broke in Alan. "She's one of the top designers at Frederick and Morrison Interiors in Beverly Hills, and it's a good firm too."

"Would you like to see some photographs of her work?" Pam eagerly pushed an album that was lying on the coffee table towards Matt.

"I sure would." Just as eagerly, Matt opened the front cover. Inside was a black-and-white publicity photo of Meg looking very poised and professional. "Lovely picture. Too bad it's not in color." He noticed that her business card was fastened next to the photo. *Bingo!* Matt filed away that bit of information, then began turning the pages, studying the photographs. He didn't know a lot about interior design, but he could tell that Meg's work was quite good.

He paused at a picture showing what looked like an old-fashioned train depot. Pam noticed his interest and rushed to explain. "Oh, I see you've found the pediatrician's office. That was a collaboration with Meg and her friend, Rosalind. Have you met Rosalind?"

"No, I haven't, but I hope to."

"Oh, she's a lovely girl, isn't she Alan?"

"You betcha!"

Pam continued. "She visited us here once, and we met her again a couple of times when we went to L.A. Rosalind says she thinks of us as family and we feel the same way towards her. Anyway, I hope you have a chance to become acquainted."

Meg changed into the ski clothes as fast as she could. Pulling on the turquoise Lycra tights, she was glad she hadn't overindulged on her mother's cookies and that she'd had that workout with Sean at the club. She gave herself a cursory once-over in the mirror, then grabbed up her canvas bag packed with the clothes she planned to wear to dinner and ran downstairs. The less time those three had together, the better.

"I'm ready. Let's go." Meg gave each parent a quick kiss, grabbed Matt's hand and began pulling him out of the room. Matt had just enough time to get one more look at Meg's business card before saying his hurried good-byes. "Pam, Alan," he said, warmly shaking their hands, "I'm so glad I had a chance to meet you."

"Likewise, Son." Alan was beaming. "Come back anytime."

Son? Meg couldn't believe her ears. If Matt could impress her father in so short a time, what couldn't he do? It was a frightening thought.

Matt escorted Meg to his ancient Scout, loaded up her gear, and climbed in. Still pondering Matt's dazzling performance with her parents, Meg paid little attention as he took a small notebook from his vest and hastily wrote in a few lines. He put it back, then paused and studied Meg for a minute, assimilating the fact that this was the beginning of the day he had planned so carefully. He lifted his eyebrows questioningly. "To the mountain?" he asked her.

Meg shook off her apprehension. "To the mountain!" she answered, giving him a thumbs-up signal and a dazzling smile that spread to her sparkling green eyes.

Matt's breath momentarily caught in his throat. *No wonder she doesn't use that smile often,* he marveled. It was dynamite.

Both Meg and Matt had learned the art of small talk as part of their jobs, so the awkward silences that people often encounter on their first date was a threat to neither of them. "Dave told me you've skied on the mountain since you were small. Is that just cross-country or do you downhill too?"

"Both. It depends on who I'm with and what kind of mood I'm in. I chose cross-country today because it's a much more sociable mode of skiing. Also less stressful. I believe that part of our agreement was to make it a relaxing day. I keep my commitments, too," he said, reminding Meg of her earlier words to him.

Meg rolled her eyes heavenward. "Come on, now. You're not going to give me a bad time, are you? Didn't you practically promise to be on your best behavior today?"

"Practically," he admitted with a grin.

Chapter Eight

*B*rightwood, Wildwood, Zig Zag, Rhododendron. Meg mentally ticked off the names of the small settlements along Route 26 on their way up the mountain. It had been years since she last visited the area, and she found pleasure in the trip's once familiar sights. The Scout carried them through a tunnel of cedars and firs adorned in their winter dress of white, and over babbling creeks of ice-cold mountain water. Once she caught a glimpse of a white-tailed deer bounding away through the protective shadows of the trees. Meg recalled Matt's words to her father. *I figure she could use some mountain air and a chance to be reminded what a great state this is.*

Presently, Matt turned his truck onto a side road and into a sno-park. "This is where we start," he announced, pulling into a parking space. They both got out and Matt surveyed the overcast sky, making note of the moderate wind. "I suggest we start out wearing jackets and wind-pants. If you don't mind carrying a pack, we can shed them later if we get too warm.''

''Sounds good. Can I help you unpack the truck?''

''Thanks. I'll take you up on that in a couple of minutes. Let's layer up first.'' They pulled on their extra clothing and Matt began rearranging the gear. ''Okay, our packs are ready. I'm glad to see you remembered your sunglasses. Here's some sunblock for you; I imagine you burn easily. Do your boots fit?'' Meg nodded. ''Good. Let's get the skis down.''

Meg and Matt trudged across the parking lot to a snow-covered road. ''I'd like to practice here first. I know you've done downhill, but cross-country is a little different. Let me demonstrate. First, hunch over and round your back like a gorilla. Let me see you do it.'' Meg hunched over her skis. ''That's good. Okay now, put pressure on your right ski as you slide it forward, now pressure on your left and slide it forward. We call that 'kick and glide.' '' Meg gave it a try. It seemed simple enough. ''Keep that gorilla hunch. Now put down your poles.''

''You're crazy,'' Meg complained.

''Trust me on this. You'll get a much better sense of balance this way. Now, we're going to add our arms to the movement. Left arm goes forward with the right ski. Right arm goes forward with the left ski. Let's do it together. I'll ski just ahead and to the side so you can copy what I'm doing. Kick, glide, kick, glide. That's right. Remember to put pressure on the ski that's advancing. Good! Let's go back and get our poles. We'll practice some more on the slope up ahead.''

Meg was glad she'd checked out a cross-country video the day before and had studied it carefully, even practicing the movements on the living-room carpet. She felt at a distinct disadvantage with this man who purportedly knew so much about the sport, and she hated the thought of making a fool of herself.

"How are you doing?" he asked as she caught up with him.

"No problems," she said cheerily. "I'm no pro, but I'll catch on."

"That'a girl."

Meg's jawline hardened. Memories of Matt's patronizing behavior on the plane came back to her. Maybe this little adventure wasn't such a good idea after all, but it was too late now. Meg pushed forward, setting as fast a pace as she could.

Matt skied beside her, glancing at her quizzically. "Hey, what's the rush?" he finally asked. "You're going to tire yourself out before we're halfway there!"

"I don't want to be a drag to you."

Matt stopped in his tracks and grabbed her arm. "Let's get one thing straight—we're here to have a good time. Not to win some kind of race. So slow down so I can keep up with you."

Meg smiled sheepishly. "Sorry."

They began skiing forward again. "See over there?" Matthew pointed off to the right to a break in a stand of trees. "That's the trail we want to take. Now the *real* fun begins." Meg felt a knot in her stomach. What did Matthew mean by 'fun'? Would she look like an idiot? Together, Matt and Meg moved onto the trail. Meg struggled to maintain her rhythm as they began a slight incline. Kick, glide, kick, glide. She dug her poles in a little deeper. The track was just wide enough for the two of them to ski side by side.

"This is what I like best," Matt exulted, "skiing on a tree-lined trail with no one else around."

Meg glanced up at the tall, snow-covered trees, at the

rocks and bushes that were now gentle mounds beneath their unsullied blankets of snow. The wind had died down, and there was no sound other than their deep, steady breathing. Together they drank in the silence.

"Did you know that the Inuits of Alaska have dozens of words for snow?" Matt asked her. "The snow up in these trees is called *qali*. It means snow that rests in the arms of trees."

"Very poetic." Meg's eyes were alive with interest. "I wonder if they have a name for the stuff we're skiing on."

"I'm sure they do, but I don't know it. Around here, it's known as 'cascade concrete.' "

"Well, it's certainly not powder, but it seems pretty good to me. Why such an awful name?"

"Hey, I'm just giving you a report. It's sure great for snowballs." Matt stopped, bent down and scooped up some snow. He packed it into a ball and faced Meg with a mischievous look.

Meg spread her hands out in front of her face. "Point-blank. No fair!"

"Aw, gee," he complained in a small-boy voice and lobbed it at a tree, missing the trunk by a good ten inches.

Meg's laughter peeled through the stillness. "Looks like I didn't have much to fear."

Matt smiled ruefully. "You've found me out. Baseball was never my strong suit. I'm better at pointing a camera." He gazed up at the sky and noticed that the clouds were clearing. "Come on. I've got something to show you." They set off again and rounded a bend. Before them stood Mt. Hood in all her snow-covered majesty. The morning sun had broken its way through the clouds just enough to train a giant spotlight on the mountain top, throwing its craggy features into high relief. Meg stopped, transfixed, as if drawn in by some magic spell cast by the mountain. Matt, too, paused to pay homage.

"Indian legend has it that Mt. Hood is a character they call Wy'east. Beneath that cool exterior, he's capable of some pretty strong emotions. Long ago, they say, he had a battle with Mt. Adams and knocked off his head. It's just a legend, of course, but I must admit, I share the natives' respect for this mountain." Matt brought out the camera he'd been carrying and took a couple of shots. "It seems like I've photographed Hood from just about every angle and in all kinds of light, but the results of each print are totally unique."

"Are you ready to press on?" he asked Meg presently. "We'll stop again at the lake over there." Matt pointed down the hill to a flat area nestling in the small valley below them.

Meg studied the rather steep slope before them. *Here goes nothing!* They began their descent. *Not bad. This is just like downhill. Whoops!* Meg, unable to make the turn, crashed headlong into a snowbank. "Darn!" she muttered.

Matt skied over to her as she lay sprawled in the snow, but instead of lending her a hand, he whipped out his camera. "Don't you dare!" she shouted furiously. Meg quickly gathered some snow, squeezed it between her gloves and fired at him. She repeated the same movement again, and then again. *Whap! Whap! Whap!*

"No! Not my camera!" he yelped. *Thump!* Her snowball had hit its target. Matt's face grew dark and angry. Meg suddenly regretted her impetuousness. She sank back into the snowbank, fearing the worst. "Why you, you . . . Little Leaguer, you!" he exploded, trying to hide the amusement that was creeping into his voice. "Where did you learn to pitch like that?"

Meg doubled over with laughter. "My brother, Sean," she gasped, tears rolling down her face.

Matt reached out his hand. Meg tugged at it in an effort to rise, only to find him tumbling toward her. "You must be heavier than you look!" he teased as he landed beside her.

"All right! That does it!" she yelled, really getting into the spirit of things as she covered his face with snow.

"You know what you get for that?" he growled, his face only inches from hers.

"No! What?" Meg's cheeks were flushed and her eyes glittered with challenge.

"This!" Matthew grabbed her braid and pulled her even closer to him. They glared at each other, nose to nose, chests heaving with exertion. Then, ever so slowly, Matt lowered his lips to hers, kissing her tenderly, and then with growing passion, warming her cool lips and stirring pleasant sensations. Matt drew back and they searched each other's faces for a long moment. *Take it slow, Matt. You've got all day.*

"I didn't realize what peril I was in when I tangled with the likes of you," he said lightly, pulling himself to a standing position, then helping Meg up. "Our lunch will be getting cold soon. We'll stop to eat when we reach the lake." Meg brushed herself off, feeling rather like a schoolgirl caught kissing in the cloakroom: guilty yet exhilarated. They proceeded down the trail without further mishap.

As they drew nearer to the lake, Matt pointed to a small white mound protruding above its surface. "See that little hump over there? That's a beaver lodge. If we look, we might see where they've chewed off a few trees." The two of them continued skiing slowly along the shore of the lake, eyes alert.

"There's our evidence, Matt. Look at that small tree

stump over there.'' Meg gestured to a thin alder stump sticking up out of the snow. ''It looks like it's been filed by a giant pencil sharpener.''

''Those beavers have been busy all right. You can see their teeth marks.''

Remembering pictures she'd seen in *National Geographic*, Meg could imagine the beaver family snuggled safely in its underwater den.

''Shall we eat over here?'' Matt motioned to a nearby clearing by a stand of trees where they would have a good view of the mountain.

''Fine by me. I know we haven't gone very far, but I'm starved!''

''Me too. Take off your skis and we'll make a seat.'' Matt placed their four skis parallel to one another, then partially unfolded a silver space blanket and placed it on top. ''Please be seated.'' Like a proper waiter, Matt bowed to Meg and gestured toward the makeshift arrangement.

''Thank you,'' Meg said gaily.

''The soup du jour,'' he recited in haughty tones, ''is Wild Mushroom, followed by an entrée of Spicy Beef and Kraut baked in individual pockets and garnished with carrot curls. The dessert includes Japanese Oranges au Naturel and Kitchen Sink Cookies.'' Meg clasped her hands in delight as Matt bowed again before arranging the food attractively on the plates.

''This is fantastic. Do you always eat like this on your trips?''

''You're the first,'' Matt admitted. ''Your choice of drink today includes Henry's Private Reserve . . . Oregon's finest, Sparkling Cranberry Juice, and Sparkling Apple Juice. Which would you prefer?''

''The Cranberry Juice would be lovely, thank you.''

Matt opened the bottle and set it in the snow beside her,

then he picked up his camera and snapped a picture of her. "A souvenir photo for the lady."

"Matt, put that camera down and come eat."

Matt sighed. "If you insist, although it's against management rules, you know."

"Hang management! We'll make up our own rules."

"I'll drink to that," he said, toasting her with his beer.

Meg laughed and took a sip of the hot soup. "This is wonderful! My compliments to the chef," she said between spoonfuls. "You weren't exaggerating when you promised gourmet fare, were you?"

"Nope. I happen to think it's some of the best in the Northwest," he boasted.

"Did you make it?"

"Oh, no, not me! I do a little cowboy cooking when I'm out camping, and I make a mean omelette but nothing like this." He gave her an enigmatic smile.

Before long, Meg had finished the soup, polished off her hot sandwich, interspersed with more compliments to the chef, had peeled and eaten an orange, and was attacking a cookie.

"More soup, sandwiches?"

"No thank you. I'm very full." Meg puffed out her cheeks and crossed her eyes.

"Anything at all so I won't have so much to carry back?" he begged.

"Ah ha! Scratch a gracious tour guide and find an indolent packer."

Matt narrowed his eyes, then reached down as if to make a snowball, but instead of throwing it at her, he began to roll it. Meg watched in apprehension as it grew bigger and bigger. Finally, when Matt had made it twice the size of a basketball, he hoisted it over his shoulders as if to dump it on top of her.

Within a split second, Meg was standing by Matt's side, squeezing his biceps in admiration. "Why, look at those muscles; better than Charles Atlas," she cooed. "You're so strong, I'll bet you could help me build a snowman with that lovely snowball you have there."

Matt blinked, then sighed. "Well, if that's what the lady wants." He lowered the ball and began rolling it in the snow again. Meg started her own, and soon they had assembled a standard snowman. They both stood back to critique their work.

"She definitely needs a little help," Meg announced.

"She? I thought all snowmen were men."

"She's telling me she's a snow*woman*."

Matt shrugged his shoulders. "If you insist. Say, maybe that's not such a bad idea. Do I get to add to her, um, contours?"

Meg laughed. "Add away. I'm going to find her some hair." Meg walked over to the stand of trees and began pulling lichen from the lower branches. She also broke off part of a twig. Returning to Matt and Snowwoman with her booty, Meg began arranging the lichen into a fetching, yellow-green coiffure.

Matt worked busily, transforming the sculpture into a buxom figure in a sculptured bikini. "So that's how you like your women." She chortled. "I don't think I can measure up."

"Don't even try," he warned her. Matt rummaged in his pack, then headed for the lakeshore with an ax in his hand.

"What have I done?" Meg moaned.

On the edge of the lake, Matt broke away a little of the ice and retrieved a handful of small rocks. "Two for her eyes," he chanted as he carefully positioned the stones. "And one," his hand waved with a flourish, "for her belly button."

Meg eyed Snowwoman's latest additions. "Not bad," she admitted, "but she needs more work."

"This better be good."

"Just you wait," Meg replied as she gathered some snow and began shaping one arm, then the other. Presently Snowwoman emerged with both hands upon ample hips. "Hmm. Almost." Meg took a small handful of snow and shaped it into a turned-up nose, then took a V-shaped twig that she had collected, and placed it for a mouth. Snowwoman gave Meg a Clara Bow smile. "What do you think?" she asked Matt, who stood back a bit, eyeing their handiwork. Don't you think she's the most wonderful snowwoman you've ever seen in your life?"

Matt laughed happily and snapped away with his camera. "Yes, and to think . . . she's our creation."

Chapter Nine

Skiing in tandem as if they were one person, Matt and Meg spent the afternoon in a rhythm of their own. Every once in a while they stopped to admire a stand of old-growth forest, a glimpse of the mountain, a hawk overhead, the tracks of a rabbit, and to allow themselves a sip of water and bites of sweet dried apricots. It was unnecessary to speak of their enjoyment in one another; it filled the air around them.

They encountered only a few people on the trail. Matt commented on the older couple who gave their greetings as they skied by. "That's the kind of old I want to be when the time comes, with enough energy to enjoy the outdoors until the end." *And with someone I love.* The thought took him by surprise, but it felt comfortable and right. He found it easy to imagine Meg being that someone. He couldn't remember ever feeling so connected to a woman.

The shadows of the trees were spreading across the white

earth, and the snow was growing crusty as they herring-boned their way up the last hill. Matt turned to Meg. "How are you doing? About ready to see the end of the trail?"

"Just about," Meg puffed. "Are we getting close?"

"Down the other side of this hill and around the curve and we'll be back on the road where we started."

"It's been a good workout. I've really enjoyed it. I haven't had time to ski in California."

"Anytime you need a break, just give me a call."

"Don't tempt me!" Meg shook her head as if trying to resist the thought.

"But that's the whole idea," Matt explained, giving her a smile that warmed her from the inside out. They reached the top of the hill and paused. Meg took a deep breath, filling her lungs with the cool mountain air. She felt free and feather-light, as if an unnamed weight had slipped quietly off her shoulders sometime that afternoon. Experiencing an urge to express her newfound sense of release, Meg dug her poles into the snow and with a shout of "Wahoo!" shoved off down the hill.

Matt, caught by surprise, watched her for a second as she tucked her poles under her arms and assumed a crouching position over her skis, shushing down the hill. Then he, too, shoved off.

"That was great!" Meg exulted when he caught up with her. Her cheeks were glowing and her eyes sparkled with excitement.

"And you were worried about slowing *me* down!" he scolded, catching her braid and giving it an affectionate tug.

"Don't flatter me," she warned, trying to read the truth in his face. "I'm sure you usually cover this trail in half the time it took us today."

"Maybe so, but I've never had a more enjoyable time."

Meg added *fun* to her list of descriptions she could apply to Matt.

Back at Matt's Scout, they loaded up the skis and the rest of the gear. "It's too early for dinner. Would you like to go up to Timberline and sit in the bar for a little while?" Matt asked.

"That would be wonderful. I dearly love the place."

In the waning light, Matt drove up the winding road, past frozen waterfalls and more tall trees. As they rounded the last turn of the road, Meg cried out, "Oh Matt, isn't it beautiful?"

"Alpenglow," Matt murmured, as he pulled his truck to a stop. Mt. Hood's summit rose before them, infused with pink light. The snowfields were pink, the snow-covered trees were pink, the lodge was pink. They glanced at each other to confirm that they, too, were pink. Matt reached over and caught Meg's hand and held it while they sat for a moment. "Magic, isn't it?" he said softly.

"Magic."

Slowly the sun sank, leaving only the lights from the parking lot to show the way. Still hand in hand, Matt and Meg climbed the broad, snow-covered steps and entered the lower lounge. "This is a real treat, Matt. It's been a long time since I've been here." Meg walked to the giant hexagonal hearth and began to warm herself by the fire. The resident Saint Bernard lying nearby thumped his tail in greeting. Matt knelt down and scratched the animal behind one ear.

Meg knew the story of how the lodge had been built during the Great Depression by down-and-out laborers and artisans and she admired the craftsman's touch in the hand-woven draperies, the decorative iron, hooked rugs, wood carvings, the stained glass and painted murals. It was, Meg reflected, a building that could appeal to both the emotions and the intellect.

Upon reaching the upper lobby, their eyes were drawn to the apex of the structure, which rose fifty-five feet above their heads, huge beams resting on the enormous central chimney stack. Here too, fires blazed in the three walk-in fireplaces.

Meg squeezed Matt's hand and they headed for the bar overlooking the lobby. It was filled with people—some skiers, some not—talking and laughing and enjoying the ambience. Meg and Matt seated themselves in sturdy wooden chairs and smiled at one another. "What a lovely day this has been, Matt."

"I'm glad you've enjoyed yourself. I hope I can keep pleasing you. The night has only begun." His words hung in the air, heavy with meaning. Meg dropped her eyes and studied the menu. "What would you like?" he asked her.

"The mulled wine sounds good."

"I'll go get it." Matt left for the bar while Meg looked about her, engraving the details of the building into the scrapbook of her mind. Soon he returned carrying their drinks, followed by a muscular-looking young man of medium stature. "Meg, I'd like you to meet a friend of mine, Dave Olsen. Dave, this is Meg Carey."

Meg laughed with sudden knowledge. "*The* Dave Olsen of Timberline Lodge, I assume?"

"In the flesh! I'm glad to see you accepted my endorsement of Matt here. You know," he continued, eyeing Meg with frank approval, "you've always had good taste in women, Matt, but I'd say you've topped yourself this time."

Meg watched with amusement as Matt's face flooded with color. "Did I hear you say you had to get back to the bar?" Matt asked.

"Well, duty calls. Hope to see you again real soon, Meg." Dave smiled gleefully at Matt.

"And to think I trusted that guy!" Matt shook his head. "What did he tell you about me?"

"Oh, he was quite informative."

"And you believe everything he said?"

"Every word."

"Curses!" Matt sunk his face in his hands.

Meg reached over to him. "Cheer up. Maybe you can salvage your reputation at dinner."

Matt brightened. "Ah, a reprieve." He took her hands in his and brought them to his lips for a light kiss. His expression was more tender than Meg had ever seen before. A spark from his eyes seemed to leap the distance between them, the sensation more heady than the heated wine she was drinking.

Matt felt, as much as saw, the change in Meg. For the first time since meeting her, she appeared unguarded, vulnerable.

"Would you like some popcorn?" The waitress set the bowl down on their table with a thump, causing some of the golden kernels to spill over onto the tabletop. Meg jumped at the unexpected interruption and Matt clamped his jaw shut in a silent curse. Meg reached absently for a kernel and chewed on it delicately, then sipped a bit of her drink. Matt looked at his watch. "It's about time to go to dinner. Shall we?"

"Hm?" There was a vague expression on Meg's face, as if her thoughts were very far away.

"I said, let's go to dinner."

"Oh, okay." Meg responded slowly, then seemed to come around. "Oh, should I change my clothes first?"

"Not yet. We can do that when we get there."

Meg, having assumed that they would be eating at Timberline, was thoroughly confused. "When we get there?"

"Right." Matt got up and pulled back Meg's chair. "Bye Dave, see you later," Matt called to his friend as he put a proprietary hand on Meg's waist and steered her out of the bar.

"Matthew, where are we going?" Meg's thoughts had returned solidly to earth. She sat stiffly in the seat of the Scout.

Matt glanced over at her as he steered his truck down the winding road. "As I said, I'm taking you to dinner."

"If I recall, you said dinner would be at a famous lodge. I don't know any famous lodges around here other than Timberline. So where is this place?" Meg's voice was strained and heavy with accusations.

Matt sighed. "Still don't trust me, do you? Well, put your mind at rest. I promised you that I would take you home any time you wanted, and I'll keep my word. Haven't I been straight with you so far? The point is, Meg, do you trust me enough to let me show you where I'm planning to take you?"

Meg was quiet. Gradually she unfolded her arms and relaxed her posture a bit. "All right. Let's see it."

Matt nodded, and turned off the main highway onto a bumpy road, not daring to look at Meg and give her an opening for protest. Presently, he pulled up in front of a small log cabin, aglow with mellow light that reflected onto the snow. Pungent wood smoke scented the air. Matt got out of the Scout and opened Meg's door for her. He offered his elbow and Meg accepted it, never taking her eyes off the charming scene before her. As they approached the door, Meg saw that the portal was surrounded with a garland of fir boughs, realistic-looking apples, and gingerbread boys. The heavy wooden door was pierced by a window of multicolored bottle glass, and overhead hung a sign that read AABERG'S MOUNTAIN RIVER LODGE.''

Meg gasped. "Matthew, is this yours?"

Matt grinned at Meg's reaction. "Not entirely. It belongs to our family. Would you like to see the inside?"

Meg turned to look at Matt, a smile playing on her lips. "I can't say that I've heard of Aaberg's Mountain River Lodge before, but I confess you've got me curious."

Matt unlocked the door and ushered Meg inside. "Oh Matt," Meg exclaimed, a rapt expression on her face, "it's so . . . so perfect!" A blaze was crackling in the river-rock fireplace, surrounded by another gingerbread and apple garland; overstuffed furniture upholstered in woolen Pendleton blankets was placed before the fire, sturdy log tables of different sizes and functions stood about, and a tall painted chest took up one corner. Meg noticed that on either side of the room draperies were drawn across what looked like alcoves. "Are those sleeping areas?" she asked Matt. He pulled aside one of the curtains to reveal a built-in bed. "How clever! That's a Swedish convention, I believe. And that chest over there looks Swedish too. Am I right?"

"Right you are. My mother was fascinated by Dad's Swedish roots. That's why she suggested we name the place Mountain River, the English translation for Aaberg. And she insisted that we incorporate some of that heritage into this cabin when we built it. We did it as a family project when I was a teenager."

"It sounds like your parents are really dynamic people, taking you skiing at a young age, building this cabin . . ."

"Yes, they were," Matt said quietly, looking away. "My father was an attorney in Portland. Both he and my mother were avid outdoors people and active in environmental issues. They died several years ago."

"Oh, Matt, I'm so sorry."

Matt shrugged. "Life goes on. At least I've got my sisters and this place. I've learned to appreciate what I do have." He paused. "So, would you like to stay for dinner, or shall I take you home?"

Chapter Ten

"It smells tempting," Meg said, as she struggled with the decision to stay at the cabin for dinner or ask Matt to take her home. "Did your caterer prepare this meal too?"

Being with Matt this day had been a pleasure, and Meg had to admit he'd been a perfect gentleman. This was the last time she'd see him, and she wasn't at all ready to say good-bye. "Well . . . I don't know how I could pass it up, especially considering the company." Meg allowed a smile to warm her features, feeling rather contrite at causing such a fuss.

"Good!" Matt tried to hide his relief. "I'll get our bags from the truck so we can change." He hurried out and returned a few minutes later. "You can change in the bedroom over there, and I'll use the one on this side. The bathroom is between the two. Take your time."

Meg stood in the small bedroom, feeling as if she had been transported to another time and place. The room was

93

dominated by a large, four-poster bed made of peeled logs and dressed with a beautiful quilt and multiple fluffy pillows. The bed faced a small hearth where a fire burned low. In the corner of the room was an old dresser with gingerbread trim. On top of it, an oil lamp spread its warm light. Rag rugs were scattered about over the floorboards. Checked curtains covered the windows.

Meg shook her head. The place had a spell about it that was hard to deny. But it was a fantasy, all fantasy. Time to come back to reality and try to remember who she was and where she was going.

Meg stood up, peeled off her ski gear, and studied the clothing in her bag. She hadn't expected to be out on a date during her visit home, and her clothing options were limited. Thinking that they would be dining at Timberline, she'd settled on a crushed velvet skirt to wear with the soft coral sweater she'd worn on the plane. She pulled on her clothes and dabbed on a bit of her favorite perfume. Then she unbraided and brushed her hair, adding some large gold disks to her ears. Studying herself in the mirror, she found herself hoping Matt would like the result.

Emerging some minutes later, Meg discovered that Matt had set out hors d'oeuvres and glasses. Classical guitar music flowed from the stereo. "Sit down by the fire here, and I'll pour us some champagne." Matt seemed to be in his element as he expertly removed the cork from the bottle.

"Champagne?"

"Well, actually it's sparkling wine. Rachel, my caterer, likes to use Oregon products whenever she can." Matt popped the cork and filled their glasses with the ice-cold bubbling liquid. "Here's to an enjoyable evening." He lifted his glass in a toast. Meg did the same and they both took a sip.

"Very good," Meg said, studying her glass. "Your caterer . . . Rachel? . . . has chosen well."

"Speaking of Rachel, she has instructed me to present you with this evening's menu." Matt handed Meg an official-looking document. Meg studied it, admiring the calligraphy.

"Smoked Salmon and Dungeness Crab Pâté," she read aloud. "Cocktail Bread and Argyle Sparkling Wine, Spinach Salad with Hazelnut Vinaigrette. Let's see . . . it looks like the entrée is Quail Stuffed with Huckleberry Sauce. This is incredible! I couldn't have expected better at Timberline. Succulent Baby Carrots and Argyle Chardonnay, and . . . Oh Matt, this is too much! Chocolate Raspberry Cheesecake with Raspberry Sauce for dessert! I happen to think that is the most divine combination of foods in the whole world. But I'm afraid I'll be too full by the time we get to it."

Matt's eyes took on a mischievous glint. "Well," he said, "we could have dessert first, I suppose."

Meg laughed. "We could, but we won't. I don't want to miss out on any of it."

"Spoken like a real trooper."

"I know. I make such sacrifices!" Meg handed Matt a slice of bread she'd covered with the pâté, helped herself too, and propped her feet up on the coffee table. Grinning at Matt, she took another sip of wine. "If this is how TV reporters spend their leisure time, I'm impressed."

Matt's reaction was pure amusement. He lifted his glass in another toast. "Here's to the glamour jobs."

"To the glamour jobs," Meg echoed.

It looked like Meg was beginning to thaw and Matt was encouraged. "I'll be back in a minute," he told her. "I think it's just about time for the next course."

Meg started to get up. "Let me help."

"Sorry. No can do. This is your night to relax. It will only take me a minute anyway. Rachel has given me precise instructions on how to assemble this."

Meg felt a sudden stab of resentment toward this Rachel person. He seemed to be very well acquainted with her, and Meg was surprised to discover that she was none too pleased about that. She began to wonder if there was anyone serious in Matt's life. According to Dave, Matt didn't have any difficulty in attracting women. And whose ski outfit had she worn all day? Meg got up from the couch and began wandering restlessly around the room.

Pausing in front of a bookcase, she began examining the books. A framed photograph caught her eye and she picked it up. Five smiling faces stared out at her. She recognized Matt as a gangling teenager with probably his two sisters and their parents. They were posing in front of the cabin and all were dressed in ski clothes. *A handsome, happy family.* A feeling of compassion for Matt came over her. Even though her relationship with her own parents was a rocky one, she couldn't imagine them no longer being there. Meg walked into the kitchen as he was pouring the vinaigrette on the salads. She watched him sprinkle a few ground nuts on the top with a flourish. "Tell me about your sisters, Matt."

"My sisters? Let's see. Sarah is the older; she's twenty-six and has her own floral design business. She did the Christmas decorations here in the cabin and she's in charge of keeping the interior in shape."

"And your younger sister?"

"She's twenty-three. It's her job to stock the kitchen here."

"And does she have a career?"

"Yes."

"Well, aren't you going to tell me?"

Matt grinned. "She's a caterer."

"And her name is Rachel!" Meg felt an immense sense of relief.

"Yup. And I'm proud of both of them."

"As well you should be. You know," Meg said, her voice soft, "I have a strong feeling your parents would be proud of all three of you."

"Thanks," he said, clearly pleased.

When Matt reflected back, their meal together seemed like a dance; a waltz, slow and sweet. They ate leisurely by fire and candlelight, the talk and laughter flowed. There was no waiter to eavesdrop or hurry them along to the next course, and Matt saw to it that the fire and music continued uninterrupted.

The food was a delight, and somehow Meg managed to squeeze a piece of cheesecake into her slender body. She couldn't remember being as relaxed in a long, long while. "It's a good thing I don't have the opportunity to eat like this every day," she confessed to Matt. "I'd begin to look like our snowwoman in no time."

Matt gave her an indulgent smile. "It's our reward for exercising so hard today. Now you go sit by the fire while I clear the table."

"Nothin' doin'," Meg drawled in her best John Wayne accent. "We're handlin' this as a team."

"Whatever you say, Podner," Matt answered, not wanting to spoil things with an argument. In ten minutes the table had been cleared and the leftovers put away. Meg began to tackle the dirty dishes. "Leave those," he commanded, taking her by the hand and leading her back to the fire.

Meg followed docilely after him and sank down on the sofa. Matt put his arm around her. She closed her eyes, feeling at peace with the world, surrounded by the wonderful smells of cedar, the sounds of the crackling fire, the warmth of Matt's arm encircling her. Alpenglow, fire-glow—it seemed to Meg that the day had been infused with magic. It had been the most fun she had had in ages. And a little romance made it even more delicious. There had been precious little time for those extras in her life these past few years. A tiny voice in the back of Meg's mind beckoned to her, but she paid it no heed.

Matt shifted his weight toward her, and with his free hand, began to trace her delicate cheekbones. Meg's eyes fluttered open in time to see him drawing near for a kiss, then closed again in surrender. The kiss drew Meg into some inner sanctum. It was so right, being here with him in this place, in his arms. She couldn't remember the last time she'd felt so relaxed, so safe, so cherished. She found herself returning his kiss with growing fervor. Let the world go away. Let herself enjoy this fantasy for just one night. What did it matter that, in reality, he and she were worlds apart.

Reality—her career—the life she'd established for herself—her dreams of success. Where was this night leading? It was contradictory to everything she thought she wanted. She couldn't get involved—not now—not with him. The tiny voice grew to a roar.

Meg's eyes flew open. "No!" she blurted, breaking off their kiss.

The urgency of her voice sent a wave of alarm through Matt. Fearing he had somehow hurt her he instinctively tightened his arm around Meg in a protective gesture.

She struggled to free herself from his suffocating embrace. "Matt, I'm sorry. I think it's time to go now." She sat on the edge of the sofa like a cat, ready to flee. She had worked too long and fought too hard for her freedom and she wasn't ready to give it up, to be dissuaded from her dreams, even by such a man as this.

"What are you talking about?" Matt lifted his hand to touch her face again, but she raised her own to intercept it.

"You promised you would take me home any time I asked. Well, I'm asking."

"Now?" he asked incredulously.

"Now!" Ice dripped from her response.

"What happened? I thought we were having a good time. Was I wrong for wanting to kiss you? Tell me," he said softly. "How do I reach you?"

"Don't waste your time, Matt. You're what we in L.A. call a 'GU,' a geographical undesirable. I have my home and career in L.A., you have yours here in Oregon. We had a fun day together and now it's time to go our separate ways."

"Why don't you move back to Oregon? Isn't this really your home?" He couldn't let her go now.

"L.A. is where I belong. To rephrase an old cliché, 'North is North and South is South, and never the twain shall meet.' "

"But we did meet," he reasoned.

Meg's laugh was harsh. "A mere accident, soon to be amended."

Matt got to his feet, his arms held stiffly by his sides, his hands doubled into fists in barely contained anger. "You're right, Meg," he said through clenched teeth. "It was all an accident, a big mistake. Go back to L.A. where you belong. Your blood is too cold for this climate."

"Just call me the Ice Princess," she replied through clenched teeth.

Chapter Eleven

Tense is barely an adequate word to describe the long drive back to Hazel Creek that dark night. Meg had insisted on helping Matt clean up the dishes while they waited for the fire to die down so they could safely lock up the cabin. Both of them felt like the beautiful mountain they had admired earlier that day—ice-cold on the outside, seething volcanoes underneath. Because Meg and Matt were civilized creatures, they refrained from further outbursts, but there was black murder in their hearts.

Dangerous was the word that came to mind when Meg thought of Matt and his mood that night, and she added it to her list. But it wasn't just his disposition that had frightened her; it was the fact that she had been so susceptible to his charm.

"Meg, is that you?" Mother called from her bedroom as Meg headed toward her own room.

"Yes, Mother." Meg paused at her mother's partially opened door.

"Come in, Dear, and tell me about your day." Mother was sitting up in bed reading, and she patted the space beside her as Meg entered. Meg sat down and smiled, trying to conceal her misery. Pam eyed her daughter. "Meggie? Do you want to tell me about it?"

Tears sprang unbidden to Meg's eyes and she looked away, fighting for composure. "Oh Mother," she said raggedly, "the Ice Princess has won again."

"Do I know this Ice Princess?"

"I'm afraid so." Meg smiled weakly through her tears.

"The Ice Princess . . . I gather you don't like her very much?"

"I thought I liked her. In fact, I've been quite proud of her ever since Toby Harris discovered her. But after tonight . . ."

"I take it you resisted Matthew's interest in you. Are you sorry?"

"No, I'm not sorry! It's just that . . . we were having such a good time together, and then . . . and now . . ." Meg laughed an ironic little laugh. "I don't even know why it bothers me. I wasn't planning on seeing him again anyway." She tossed her head impatiently, her hair swaying.

Pam frowned and removed her reading glasses. "Let me get this straight. You spent the day with Matthew, had a great time, but even before you had your, ah, your disagreement, you had written him off?"

"Well, yes . . ."

"Why?"

"Why?" Had Meg forgotten, or was this a new side of her mother? Pam's questions were every bit as blunt as the rest of the Careys'. "What difference does it make?"

"Meggie, ever since you were small, you've always

seemed to know what you wanted, and although you may not believe this, I've tried to stand on the sidelines and let you handle life your own way. But I suspect where Matthew is concerned, you don't have a clue.''

"Oh! So I should just fall head over heels for him and forget about the plans and dreams I have for my life!"

"Meggie! That's not what I'm trying to say and you know it! It's just that falling in love doesn't always happen on schedule. It can't be plugged into a five-year plan."

"I rejected Matthew because he's chauvinistic, insensitive, and . . . and . . .''

"In the same category as Toby Harris?" Pam asked, a smile tugging at her mouth.

"Definitely!"

Pam smiled with affection at her stubborn daughter. "Well, I certainly don't want you dating a guy like that. But I do want you to be open to the possibility of love when it comes your way." She patted her daughter's hand.

Meg sighed. "I know." There was silence as Meg studied a flower on the bedspread and chewed on her lip.

Pam lifted Meg's chin with her hand and gave her daughter a critical gaze. "There's something else bothering you. Tell me about it."

Meg studied her mother's face, trying to gauge the impact of her unspoken question. She swallowed, keeping new tears at bay. "At the courts the other day, Sean reminded me of the times you put me in the coat closet. Why did you do that?"

Pam closed her eyes for a moment. "Oh, Meggie, I'd hoped you'd forgotten. It's not something I'm very proud of." She leaned her head back against the headboard and took a deep breath before continuing. "When Gram and Granddad Carey retired from the ministry and moved in with us, there were times when I thought I'd go out of my mind. Your grandfather believed in the absolute authority of parents, and you, Meg, had such a hard time keeping still and acting like the 'little lady' he thought you should be. I'm ashamed to admit it, but I was so concerned about Granddad's approval, that I tried to discipline you much more than I would have otherwise. Maybe because of that, you had terrible temper tantrums. They got so bad, that I took you to a child psychologist who suggested I put you in a room by yourself until you calmed down.

"I was afraid that if I shut you in the bedroom you and Sean shared you'd break some of his things, so I had you sit in the closet. I know now that it was a terrible mistake. Can you ever forgive me?"

Meg was too full of emotion to speak, so she leaned over and gave her mother a long hug. "It's okay now, Mom. I love you," she was finally able to whisper.

It was with mixed feelings that Meg said good-bye to her parents the next day. Her relationship with her father hadn't changed much, but she felt encouraged by the growing understanding with her mother. They both waved as they stood side by side on the front stoop, watching Meg drive out of sight and on to the airport.

There was no Matt to hold her hand while she waited for takeoff, but his words of advice remained with her, comforting and guiding her. Despite her anger, she couldn't be sorry he'd been there when she needed him. Meg took a slow, deep breath.

"Meg, I'm so glad you're back!" Rosalind rushed up and gave Meg a huge hug as she made her way to her desk Tuesday morning.

"Rosalind, you sound desperate. Did I leave you with that big a mess?" Meg pulled back and looked at her friend. Rosalind's usually happy face was marred by dark shadows under her eyes. "Rosalind, what's happened?" Meg said in alarm.

"Oh everything's fine here, just fine," Rosalind replied in a flat voice, attempting a smile. "The Warren job in New York came through for you. The contract is up at the front desk. And I'm working on a major remodel on a house out in Malibu. Business is booming."

Meg heaved a sympathetic sigh. "Then it's got to be personal. Men to be specific. Man to be superspecific. Are you free for lunch? Can we talk about it then?"

"A shoulder to cry on? Darn! I'm so tired of this stupid dating game."

"That makes two of us. We've got a lot to talk about."

Rosalind seemed to pull herself together. "Okay. How about lunch. Eleven-forty-five?"

"That's good. By the way, is Phillip around?"

"I just saw him in the drafting room."

"Great. See you later."

Meg found Phillip deep in blueprints. "Phillip? Hi. Can I talk with you for a minute?"

"Sure, Meg. Hey, looks like you survived your vacation."

"Better and worse than I imagined. Say, Phillip, I know you've taken a class or two at UCLA in dream interpretation. Do you think you could help me figure out a dream I had while I was in Oregon?"

"Well, I don't know. I'm not a licensed psychologist, but I might be able to help you."

"It's funny, Phillip, but I think I've worked some of it out already. Still, I'd just like to get clear about it all, if I can. Could you stay a little after work? I'll have a pizza delivered, goat cheese and lamb sausage, your favorite."

"On a whole wheat crust, with Greek olives?"

"You got it. I'll have it here just after six. Thanks a lot, Phillip."

Meg and Rosalind sat in the little bistro across the street from their workplace, waiting for their lunch to be served. "I gather your Christmas vacation didn't go exactly as planned, Rosalind."

Rosalind winced. "Talk about an understatement," she said. "No, as you know, I was all set to go skiing at Mammoth with Zack. I guess I should have expected something when he told me he couldn't see me on Christmas Day . . ."

"Do you mean you spent Christmas alone?"

"Yes, but that wasn't the worst of it. Zack didn't even call Christmas or the next day to see how I was doing. Would you believe, I had to call him to find out when we would be leaving? When I finally got him, he sort of hemmed and hawed around, and then he said . . . get this: 'Rosalind, I'm just not good enough for you. You'd be better off without me.' "

"What a rat! Oh Roz, I'm so sorry! You must feel terrible." Meg frowned in sympathy for her friend.

"It was a pretty big blow, all right. But now that I look back on it all, there were a lot of little problems that I guess I just didn't want to see." Rosalind morosely studied her glass of iced tea.

"I guess it's no good trying to make a relationship work when it's really not meant to be." Meg smiled perfunctorily at the waiter who set a plate of food in front of her.

"I'm sorry!" said Rosalind. "I've been so preoccupied with my problems, I didn't ask how it went for you at your folks."

"Strange. Very strange. I had a blowup with Dad. Things with Mother are pretty good. Eliza Jane and I had a great time, and I . . . I met someone on the plane, but . . ."

"But what? Meg, tell me! Is he good-looking? Are you

going to see him again?'' Rosalind's eyes lit up for the first time that day.

''Well, there isn't much to tell. I went cross-country skiing with him, but we ended up having a fight. I'm glad I found out right away that he's not the one for me.''

''Too bad. I was hoping that at least you had gotten lucky.'' Rosalind sighed. ''So, where do we go from here?''

''Back to work, my dear.'' Meg blotted her lips briskly with her napkin and shoved her plate away, a purposeful look on her face. ''I have a New Year's prediction; you and I are going to make it big this year, maybe even make the cover of *The Designer's Magazine*.''

Rosalind laughed. ''That's what I like about you Meg. Besides being a hard worker, you are an optimist and a dreamer . . . and my best friend.'' She lifted her glass. ''Here's to the successful careers of Meg and Rosalind, *designers par excellence!*''

Meg laughed too. ''To Meg and Rosalind, the hottest design team in L.A. The nation. No, the world!'' They left the restaurant laughing. It felt good to be back on track again. ''Let's try to work together on the next project,'' Meg suggested to her friend.

''Yes, let's. It's about time we did that again.''

The afternoon flew by for Meg as she immersed herself in her work: making plans for her trip to New York, wrapping up loose ends on old projects, checking on potential new work that she and Rosalind could share. Work had always been her salvation, and today it seemed even more so. If she was as cold-blooded as Matt thought, then she would use that trait to her best advantage. She would function like an efficient machine and reap the rewards. It was nearly six when she remembered to send out for the pizza. Already her family, Oregon, and Matt were receding into obscurity. Still, it would be a good idea to have Phillip help her wrap up the vacation in a neat package. Then she could be truly free to move on.

"... then I realized I had actually killed the intruder because he was stealing Mother's china." Meg concluded her account of her dream to Phillip.

Phillip leaned back in his chair, licking the last bit of pizza from his fingers. "Mmm. Interesting. How did you feel when you realized you'd done him in?"

"I felt awful ... guilty. I kept asking myself what I could tell the police, but I just couldn't come up with an explanation to justify it." Meg was sitting across from Phillip, her shoeless feet propped up on another chair.

"So, you felt guilty in killing him, even though he was stealing something that your mother valued?"

"Yes. Although the china was important to her, I realized it held little value for me."

"Tell me more about the china, Meg."

"Well ... It's very lovely. It's been there in the cupboard as long I can remember. When we were kids, my mother told us never to touch it. It was dear to her, although I doubt that it was very valuable, monetarily anyway."

"Did you want that china, Meg?"

"You know what's funny? Mom gave me one of the pieces for a Christmas present this year. I couldn't believe she'd part with any of it. I've placed the vase in an honored spot in my apartment, but it doesn't really go with anything else I own."

"So you treasure the china because it's part of your family heritage ..."

"Yes. It's not really my style, though."

"Could you say the same thing about your mother?"

Phillip made a tent of his fingers and pressed them thoughtfully to his lips.

"You mean, do I treasure my mother because she's my mother?"

"Yes, even though you seem to have a different set of goals?"

"Well, it's true . . . Mother never had a career, married when she was quite young, had babies right away, goes to church every Sunday, visits the shut-ins . . . you know, the perfect wife and mother."

"And that's not the way you want to live your life."

"No! I wouldn't be here doing what I'm doing if I wanted to be just like her."

"Good. So we've established that the china is like your mother's value system . . . something to be appreciated but not to be desired for yourself."

"Right. So that explains why it wasn't right for me to kill that man. He couldn't really steal Mother's values from me, because they weren't mine." Meg was beginning to enjoy this little game.

"From what you told me earlier, you're quite concerned with the discrepancy between what your mother wants for you and what you want."

"I guess my dream was about knowing my own mind and not being so concerned about what my family thinks. Funny, I thought I'd resolved that already."

"It takes most of us a while to develop an adult-to-adult relationship with our parents, Meg. It's not a matter of accepting or rejecting their values; it's making a conscious choice for ourselves, examining our own hearts and minds."

"You're pretty wise." Meg smiled.

"Hey, I'm learning right along with you. In fact, I think

I'll call my dad tonight. There's something I'd really like to talk with him about.''

"Good. Well, I suppose that about takes care of it. I'll just have to be aware of where my thoughts and actions are coming from: make sure they're from my own heart and not a reaction for or against other people's standards.''

"Simple, isn't it?''

"Phillip, I really want to thank you. You've been a big help.'' Meg picked up the empty pizza carton and began stuffing it efficiently in the trash can. As she did so, an image of the puzzle box came back to her. Tonight she'd managed to stuff one more piece of her life into that box. It felt good to tidy up.

Phillip continued reclining in his chair. A bemused look gathered on his face. His next words froze her in her tracks.

"So, tell me Meg, what would you have done if it had been your china?''

Chapter Twelve

Meg couldn't get Phillip's question out of her head. True, it was only a dream, but what if the thief had threatened her own values? Would she have been justified in killing him? Is this what she had done to Matt? Had she overreacted? Matt had challenged her carefully crafted life: her wealthy clients, her desire to separate herself from Oregon and family. He'd stirred her emotions to a level she didn't like to admit. But she'd written him out of her life, so why couldn't things return to normal? She thought about it as she drove from her work in Beverly Hills to her home in Venice. She thought about it as she puttered aimlessly around her apartment. She thought about it as she soaked in the tub, her legs dangling over the edge. She thought about it as she crawled into bed, knowing that the chance for sleep was thin. She couldn't stop thinking about it: the dream and Matthew.

If only she had had an alternative other than banishing

him or giving in. Sadly, there were no options with Matt. She just wished that her victory over her emotions hadn't left her with the taste of defeat in her mouth and her heart feeling as empty and hollow as a rusty tin can. Meg gradually fell into a restless sleep, her head full of twisting images, her heart full of turbulent emotions.

Consumed with righteous anger over Meg's behavior, Matt left for location with his camera crew early Monday morning. His mood had been as black as the lowering sky, and the trip had been a disaster. Their government-issued van had a flat tire, buckets of rain poured down on them, one of the cameras jammed, the deer they were trying to film had proven elusive—the only shots had been of trees and the wily animals' rumps bounding away through the forest. The crew had been sullen, a reflection of the weather, he supposed.

It wasn't until Matt sat in the projection room reviewing takes of the outing that the ludicrousness of it all suddenly struck him and he burst out laughing—laughing until the tears rolled down his cheeks and his sides ached—laughing until he was weak and washed clean of the pain and anger he'd been holding tightly in his gut. He supposed that if anyone at the station had seen his fit, management would have insisted upon placing him on leave until he regained his sanity. It was odd, but the laughter seemed to be a giant step in his recovery. He felt as if he'd been reprieved from hell.

To be sure, Matt's ego had suffered a bruise the size of a shoe, ladies ten narrow to be exact. He was astonished to discover that Meg could hurt him so.

The challenge had been to find out more about her, to convince her to let down her guard. It was obvious that his usual approach with women wouldn't work with her. Matt closed his eyes and pictured her laughing face as she launched a snowball at him, the little-girl delight when she saw the cabin, the reflective soul as she gazed out over the sparkling landscape, the scent of her hair. He'd achieved a measure of success with her, but in the end he'd blown it.

He hadn't had to work at a relationship before; they had all been rather casual, friendly. The women just sort of drifted in and eventually drifted off. He'd never thought much about it until now. If there didn't happen to be a woman in his life when he needed female companionship, his sisters were always there to lend an ear, fix a good meal, joke with him. And he was a busy man. For Pete's sake, he was out on assignment for half of each week. He couldn't expect a woman to put up with that kind of schedule indefinitely. Not that he'd ever bothered to ask.

Which didn't solve his dilemma over Meg. It occurred to him that perhaps what she needed was a real courtship—a bit old-fashioned—but it might work. What did it matter that she was as mad as hell at him right now or that she lived hundreds of miles away?

The rest of the week had proven to be a blessed whir of activities for Meg: telephone conferences with the Warrens, calls to colleagues who might be able to recommend New York tradesmen, a review of the current town house floor plan and sketches for remodeling, stolen moments of shopping for the proper New York clothing, and a game of racquetball with Rosalind. Meg's plans were to leave Saturday morning so that she'd have a day in the city to catch her breath and analyze her strategy. It was late Friday afternoon, and just about everything on her list had been accomplished. She was deep in discussion with her boss, Madeline Frederick, when her phone rang. It was Sue, the receptionist. "Meg, there's a gentleman at the front desk to see you."

Meg sent an apologetic look to Madeline as she answered. "I don't have any appointments this afternoon, Sue. In fact I'm planning on leaving shortly. What did he say his name is?"

"He hasn't told me, Meg." Sue's voice was almost a whisper. "He says he's a friend of yours."

"Tell him he'll have to wait for a few minutes. I've got some business to wrap up with Madeline."

"Okay, but if I were you, I wouldn't keep a guy like this waiting too long."

"Thanks Sue." Meg tried not to show her irritation.

Rosalind eyed the tall, attractive man who was pacing the reception area. She'd gotten a mysterious call from Sue, telling her she had an unnamed visitor up front. Vendors and clients were usually long gone by this time of day, especially on a Friday. She glanced questioningly at the receptionist who, in silent answer, inclined her head towards the man. Rosalind stepped forward and extended her hand. "Hi. I'm Rosalind Stewart. You wanted to see me?"

"Hello, Rosalind. I'm Matthew Aaberg. I'm waiting for Meg, and I wanted to meet you while I had the chance. I've heard so much about you, from Meg of course, and Pam and Alan too."

"Oh, are you from Oregon, Mr. Aaberg?"

"Matt. Yes, I'm from Oregon, and I happened to be in town so I thought I'd drop by. Nice office you have here." He glanced around to show his interest.

"Is this your first visit? Maybe you'd like a little tour while you're waiting for Meg?"

"I'd like that."

* * *

". . . and that's about it, except for Meg's office, of course. Let me peek in and see if she's free now." Before Matt could stop her, Rosalind entered Meg's office, pulling him behind her. "Meg, look who I've brought to see you!" Meg was absorbed in loading papers into a briefcase. Matt's pulse raced at the sight of her. She looked more beautiful than ever. As he stood admiring her, Meg looked up and her mouth flew open. She blanched, then turned scarlet.

"You!" she gasped.

"Right, as always," Matt said cheerfully. He made a move to sit down on one of the chairs.

"I don't remember inviting you here. Haven't I made it clear that I don't ever want to see you again?"

Matt froze in mid movement, then relaxed his stance and settled with conspicuous ease into the chair. "Guess not," he said.

Rosalind watched the scene with amazement. "Uh, excuse me," she muttered. "I have to get back to my desk."

Matt and Meg stood with eyes locked on each other. Neither one paid Rosalind any attention as she backed carefully away.

As soon as Rosalind was gone, Matt let the pleasant smile slip from his face. "Meg, I know you don't want to see me . . ."

"You've got that right!"

". . . but I came to apologize," he continued. "I acted like a damn fool when you asked me to take you home, and I want you to know I'm very sorry. Can we talk about it?" Matt's eyes were filled with pleading.

"I doubt if there's anything left to say," she stammered, thrown off guard. The last thing she'd expected from him was an apology—and in person.

"Maybe not, but can we at least find out?"

"I don't have much time. I'm leaving for New York City in the morning." Meg felt her resolve weakening.

"Let me take you out to dinner. You have to eat. Remember what that book on flying says about eating a good meal before a flight?" A hopeful smile played on his lips.

"No!" Meg took a deep breath and ran her fingers shakily through her hair. "I mean . . . how about a walk on the beach instead? Your book said it's also important to exercise."

"Anything you say!" The fact that she'd read the book was encouraging.

"But first I'll have to stop at my apartment in Venice to start a load of wash. Do you mind?"

"Sounds good. I've got my rental car parked across the street. I'll follow you."

Matt could hardly contain his feelings of exaltation as he followed Meg's car. He knew that all had not been forgiven, but at least he had another chance. He promised himself he wouldn't screw up this time.

As they pulled up to the apartment complex, Meg motioned to a parking space, then disappeared into a subterranean garage. She reappeared a few minutes later with a number of packages in her arms. "I'll trade you," he called as he sprinted up to her. In his hand was a long-stemmed red rose.

Meg blushed, chagrined at her pleasure over the offering.

"Maybe we'd better put it in some water. It's been sitting in my car for awhile."

"Yes, sure. This way." Meg led Matt to her door and opened it. She snapped on a few lights and disappeared into the kitchen. "Just make yourself at home," she said over her shoulder.

Matt put down the packages, stuffed his hands in his

pockets, and wandered around the living room intently studying the coolly sophisticated furnishings. Neoclassical chairs were pulled up to a glass-topped, marble-based dining table, a sleek, black and white striped couch was accompanied by a side table whose feet were carved to resemble lion's paws. The room looked untouched and devoid of color, more like a stage setting than a place to live in. Then Matt spied a basket of knitting tucked behind the couch. He smiled.

Meg returned from the kitchen with a frown on her face. "I can't seem to find an appropriate container. Would you mind if I made the stem shorter?"

"It's yours now. Do with it as you please."

Meg picked up a lovely old-fashioned vase from a white marble shelf in the dining area, and took it back into the kitchen. "There," she said with satisfaction as she returned again and placed the vase with the rose back on the shelf. "That looks just right, doesn't it?"

"Just right. Now if you'll excuse me, I'll get changed."

Meg stared blankly at her closet for a few moments, trying to gauge the import of Matthew's appearance. Pulling herself together, she changed into jeans and a sweatshirt and gathered up the clothing to be washed. When she had finished her tasks, she returned to Matt in the living room.

"I'm ready," she said cheerily, trying to pretend that walking with Matt on the beach was a common event. She yanked a jacket out of the hall closet. "It's only four blocks to the beach."

They strode silently down the sidewalk. As they neared the beach, Meg's eyes fell on Annie's, a hot dog stand. Her mood shifted suddenly. "Say, how about some hot dogs?" she asked.

Matt shrugged his shoulders and grinned. "Why not?"

Meg ran up to the stand, dodging a couple of teenagers

on rollerblades who zipped by. As she ordered, Matt stood behind her and absently examined the items offered for sale. In minutes, two dogs with the works and two Cokes were slapped down on the counter.

"I'll take a package of those candies over there," Matt told the vendor.

"You have a sweet tooth," Meg teased as they headed for the boardwalk.

"Yup," he mumbled between bites of food. "I seem to be hooked."

They continued to walk and eat, saying little. When they had finished and thrown the wrappings into a trash can that stood under a streetlamp, Matt drew out the candy. He tore open the package, shook some of the sweets into his hand, and began to pick through them. Meg watched him curiously and gasped with surprise when he tossed most of them into the trash can.

"What are you doing?" she asked, laughing.

"Hold out your hand," he commanded. Meg complied and one by one he placed all the candies in her hand. There were only two colors, brown and red. Each had the letter *M* on it.

"Thank you . . . I think," she said as they walked across the sand. "What am I supposed to do with them?"

"Enjoy them," he said with a smile.

Meg glanced at him, waiting for further explanation, but he did not elaborate. She shrugged her shoulders and ate a couple.

Matt reached out for Meg's hand and held it as they strolled close to the breakers, the tang of the salt air filling their nostrils. "I can see why you like it here," Matt said, breaking the silence.

"Venice is special. It's where all kinds of people come. In the summer, it's like a festival in the afternoons. But I especially like it when it's not so crowded. Sometimes I come down here early in the morning before work when the fog is still clinging to the beach. And I love it when the storms come rolling in."

"That's your Oregon blood talking."

Meg ignored his comment. "How did you find me this time? Same old homing device?"

"The same." He grinned at her and put his arm around her shoulder, as if to protect her from the increasing breeze, mist, and darkness. "Say. That's some apartment you have. Very contemporary."

"Thank you."

"Is it really you though, Meg? It seems so kind of . . . oh I don't know . . . cold or something."

Meg took a step away from him, breaking out of his hold. "You may think so, but readers of the *Times* seemed to like it. After it was featured last year in the *Home* section, my commissions picked up considerably."

"I'm sorry, I didn't mean to offend." Matt reached for her hand again and gave it a gentle squeeze. As he did so, his palm came into contact with the ring she wore. He lifted her fingers to study the jade stone nestled in an unusual gold setting. It was the same ring he'd noticed her wearing that day on the plane. "Your ring is really quite special. It matches your eyes. Does it have a history?"

"It belonged to my grandmother," Meg answered, a smile in her voice. "Grandma Carey gave it to me when I graduated from high school, just shortly before she died."

"Your family is really important to you, isn't it? I'll bet they would love to have you back in Oregon."

"Are we going to start that argument again? I just told you, I belong here. My career is really beginning to take hold. My apartment building is turning condo soon and I'm planning to buy into it. Oregon is a part of my past, not my future.''

"I think you're making a mistake, Meg. You shouldn't run away from your past.'' Matt's brow creased in a disapproving frown.

Meg felt her stomach cave in. "Run away?'' she managed in a strangled voice. "Because I choose to make my own way in the world, independent of my family, you say I'm running away?''

"Well, it does seem that you're doing your utmost to erase reminders of your past. Look at your apartment, for instance.''

"Cold! Right?''

"Yes, cold! I thought a person's home was supposed to reflect the personality of the owner. You're not at all like that.''

"Ah! So now you're trying to tell me how to do my own decorating! I guess you've forgotten the Ice Princess. Cold, remember? *Brrrr.*'' Meg crossed her hands over her body and shook herself with exaggerated shivers, all the while staring at him angrily.

"Meg, there's no reason to get so upset.'' Matt endeavored to remain reasonable. "I'm just trying to point out that you'd probably be much happier if you came to terms with your family.''

"I can't believe this! You sound just like my father! Always telling me not to get upset, always thinking that he knows what's best for me. Well, *I* know what's best for me, and that's to have you out of my life! I'm telling you, Matthew Aaberg, so that there will be no doubt in your mind—I want you out of my life and I want you to stay out! And take your harebrained homing device with you. I don't ever want to see you again! Have I made myself clear?''

"Ice-crystal clear," Matt said grimly. "And I'll do that just as soon as I get you back to your apartment."

"Don't bother! I can take care of myself!"

"And that's just what I'm going to let you do as soon as you're back to the apartment." Matt roughly spun her around and steered her in the direction from which they had come. When they reached her building, he called to her retreating back. "Good-bye, Meg."

She didn't answer until he was out of earshot. "Good-bye forever," she said, sadness mixed with the anger.

Chapter Thirteen

Matt headed straight toward LAX and took the first
Portland-bound flight he could get. There was no point in
hanging around. It had been a bad decision to try to patch
things up with Meg. Clearly they did not have enough in common to keep their relationship afloat. He had never, in his
thirty-one years, had such difficulties with a woman. In fact,
he was surprised at himself for letting one get to him the way
Meg had.

Now that it was over, he'd be able to pull himself together. A number of possibilities presented themselves. For
the first time in years, he felt a yearning for a smoke. Or
maybe a good, roaring drunk would help. No, he wasn't
the type to enjoy self-destruction. He went over a mental
list of his latest crop of female admirers. For one reason or
another, none of them seemed to have what he wanted.
Each time he conjured up a new face, it quickly melted

away and was replaced with a picture of Meg. Well, if it was going to be like that, he'd become a monk.

It was the wee hours of Saturday morning by the time Matt reached his apartment. He stripped off his jeans and fell into bed. The minute his head hit the pillow, he was out.

Meg forced her mind to focus on the business of packing for her trip. She placed her clothes in the dryer and brought out her garment bag, laying it on the bed. Meg told herself she was glad Matt had come to see her. Their argument had left no room for hope of reconciliation, hope which had followed her from Oregon to L.A. She no longer had to figure out just where he belonged in her life—he simply didn't.

Later in the evening, Meg called Rosalind to briefly explain her behavior at the office and to say good-bye. Rosalind knew better than to question her friend any further.

As Meg prepared to leave the next morning, she paused at her front door, put her luggage down and walked back into her apartment, to the marble shelf. Without hesitating, she picked up her grandmother's vase and carried it to the kitchen, removed the rose with one smooth movement and put it in the trash. Then she was out of the door and on the street to meet her waiting taxi.

In the backseat, Meg took a deep breath, then exhaled slowly. Maybe the sole reason for her meeting Matt had been learning how to overcome her claustrophobia. It was something positive she could remember, and she would, for a little while anyway. *You'll be fine.* Meg's hands clenched as she remembered his words. Better believe she'd be fine, especially without Matthew Aaberg around to muddle her thinking. To her list she added the worst word she could think of to describe him: *patronizing.*

At Burbank Airport, Meg found her clients' 727 jet and greeted the waiting pilot. Door-to-door service—this was her idea of hassle-free flying. She settled comfortably into a leather seat in the small lounge and looked around with approval. The decor had obviously been executed by one of the several globe-hopping designers whose specialty was plane and boat interiors. It seemed that the Warrens never stinted on quality. Meg knew they had a number of homes around the world and were involved in several international business ventures. She gazed absently out the window as the pilot revved the engines. Moments later the jet screamed down the runway and sailed into the blue sky, toward New York City.

Matt woke from a deep slumber, feeling as if he'd been mugged. He groggily peered at the clock . . . 7:05 . . . A.M. or P.M.? It was dark outside. What day was it? He pulled on his jeans and, bleary-eyed, went to collect his mail. A fresh stack of *Sunday Oregonians* lay in their rack in the lobby. Sunday morning! He shook his head in amazement. He'd slept for twenty-eight hours straight. It beat the record he'd made after college finals one semester.

Matt's stomach growled and he remembered his last meal had been a hot dog on the beach with Meg. Reaching into his pocket, he drew out an empty and wrinkled brown package with two *M*'s printed on it. Mat and Meg. Redhead and dark brown. It seemed like a lifetime ago.

Back in his apartment, Matt made himself some instant coffee. He drank it while he fried up a couple of eggs and some sausage. He inspected the bread he'd planned to toast, then grimaced and tossed it in the general direction of the wastebasket. When he cooked for himself he wasn't especially picky, but a week's worth of mold was more than even he could stomach.

Periodically glancing at the clock, Matt read the news-paper and ate his breakfast. The motions were automatic and he consumed without tasting. The old, familiar restless feeling swelled in him as he thought about what to do with the day. Sundays had always been special when he was growing up—early-morning church and an outing of some sort with the family. On idle days like today, he often felt an acute vacuum, his mind and body demanding some kind of action to fill it. When his sisters were younger and Rachel was still in his care, he had carried on the family tradition. As they grew older and more independent, he had let the practice fall away. He supposed Rachel was still sleeping. Friday and Saturday nights were her busiest. What the heck. Waking her would be good for a laugh anyway. No matter how she protested, she was always a good sport.

He let the phone ring, knowing she would eventually answer it. "Hello?" Her voice sounded muffled, irritated.

"Well, hello there Sleepyhead. You gonna stay in bed all day? Now we can't have that, can we?"

"Matthew! Wait until I get my hands on you!" Crash! The receiver was dead. Matthew rang again.

"Matthew! Go away! Can't you tell I'm sleeping?"

"Make that *was* sleeping. Boy, I don't know what it is about me, but you're the second woman in the space of two days who's told me to shove off. Whatza matter? Do I have bad breath or somethin'?"

"No, it's your insensitive, opinionated, and all-around maddening personality!" There was a pause. "All right, Matt," Rachel's voice was softer now, "do you want to talk about it?"

"Talk about what? I was just remembering how we used to go places as a family on Sundays. Thought if you didn't already have plans, maybe we could, um, do something together."

"Got anything in mind?"

"Well, for starters, I could take you out to lunch."

"I might be interested," she said coyly. "What else?"

"We could go to the zoo. They've got a new rain forest exhibit that's pretty neat."

"Looks like a rain forest right outside my window."

"See any monkeys?"

"No, just talking to one."

"Thanks a lot!"

"Sorry. Old habits die hard. What time do you want to pick me up?"

"Eleven-thirty okay?"

"Sounds okay."

"Well, see you then." Good old Rachel. She'd turned out to be a pretty nice kid. Matt went off to the bathroom. He knew it was an environmental sin, but he took a long, hot shower.

Rachel and Matt sat side by side on a bench, watching the bright birds swaying in the jungle foliage that filled the new exhibit in the Washington Park Zoo. "So, she told you to go away, huh? Did she mean permanently?"

"Yeah, permanently, as in 'forever.' " Matt was hunched over, his hands clasped between his legs, staring at an invisible speck on the floor.

"I guess you feel pretty lousy about it."

"Oh, I'll get over it."

Rachel sighed. "Yes, you always do."

"What's that supposed to mean?"

"I mean, you've had lots of girlfriends, but none of them have meant enough for you to pursue seriously. So why should Meg be any different?"

"How did you know it was Meg?"

"Matthew, I'm a woman, I know these things."

"Nah, you're just a little kid." He reached over and tweaked her nose

"Matthew." There was a note of authority in her voice that he hadn't heard before. "Do you treat all women the way you treat me?"

"How do I treat you, Lambkin?" A smile played on his lips despite his attempt at seriousness.

"Like a small child who's about to beg candy. I don't know where you get it from. Dad wasn't like that with Mom. Maybe it's from the years you were parenting Sarah and me."

Matt winced. He hadn't expected this from his adoring little sister. "Hey, I work with women every day. They'd never let me get away with being a chauvinist."

"But I let you get away with it, and I bet your girlfriends have too."

"Well, that's different."

"How?"

"They aren't coworkers, they're dates. Besides, they don't seem to mind." He grinned, thinking of the women in his past.

"Maybe they don't have the brains to mind. Maybe you've never dated someone like Meg before."

Matt smote his forehead with the palm of his hand. "Too true!"

Warming to her subject, Rachel settled more comfortably on the bench. "Let's see. You've told me that Meg is about my age and a successful interior designer in Los Angeles."

"Did I tell you that?"

"Uh-huh. Now, what would you say it would take for someone her age to get to where she is?"

"Oh, I suppose talent, brains, tenacity. Those are always the key ingredients to success. Plus, maybe a little bit of luck, but I don't necessarily subscribe to that theory. I think a person usually has to make his own luck.''

''So you've told me—several times. Anyway, we've established that Meg has probably followed your formula for success.''

''All right, Sis. Get to the point.''

''Patience!'' Rachel wore the look of a determined schoolmarm ready to smack him with a ruler if he didn't behave. ''So how do you suppose she sees herself?''

Matt shrugged his shoulders. ''How should I know?''

''You do,'' she persisted. ''You're a reporter. It's your business to know those things. Now answer my question.''

''I suppose she sees herself as independent . . .''

''Good . . .''

''. . . intelligent, hard-working . . .'' a look of understanding, then consternation played across Matt's face. ''You're saying she probably didn't appreciate me giving her unsolicited advice.''

''Is that what you did?'' Rachel asked gently, resting her hand on his arm.

Matt nodded glumly.

''So, what are you going to do now?'' Rachel was suddenly all business, her tone of solicitude having vanished.

Matthew exploded and Rachel jerked her hand away in surprise. ''Nothing! It's too late. I told you, she never wants to see me again.'' He jumped up from the bench and began pacing back and forth.

''Guess you'll have to figure out how to change her mind, won't you? Figure out a way to get *her* to come to you.'' Rachel was so obviously confident in his abilities, it touched him. Nevertheless, their conversation was getting him nowhere.

''Rachel, drop it.''

She held up her hand to stay him. Matt imagined a pair

of wire-rimmed glasses perched on the end of her nose. "One last bit of advice: Ask yourself what Meg really wants from you and what you want from her. Then figure out what you have to lose or gain."

Matt couldn't suppress a smile of new appreciation for Rachel. "I think I'm going to have to start calling you *Tiger* instead of *Lambkin*. How did you get to be so smart?"

"Oh, I learned a lot from Mom, and a thing or two from my big brother, who by the way is known to be a sensitive, intelligent human being." It was all Matt could do to keep from tweaking her nose again. Old habits died hard.

Chapter Fourteen

Matt had returned. He was far away, but Meg could tell who it was by his height and broad shoulders. With his every approaching step, her sense of distress grew. Meg called to him, "Matthew!" but he didn't seem to hear her. He just kept coming nearer and nearer. Meg's chest was heaving with anger, frustration, and hurt by the time he reached her. "Matthew!" she cried again. "Listen to me!" Still no response. Then she saw that he had no ears. "No!" she uttered in shock and protest.

Meg searched his eyes, trying desperately to communicate with him, but they were not warm and loving as she'd remembered. Instead, a veil had been drawn over his face, blurring his features.

"Look at me," she begged. "It's me, Meg. It's me. Please look." But his face told her that he either couldn't or wouldn't. Meg blinked at the tears that were coursing down her face. When she opened her eyes again, she

129

gasped. The face was not Matt's at all, but had been transformed into her father's. The uncomprehending expression remained the same.

"Look at me!" she sobbed. "Listen to me!" Meg tried tearing at the veil, but her hands slipped away, unable to grasp it. Desperately, she clawed at thin air, trying to penetrate the barrier that separated them. "Look at me! Listen to me! Look at me! Listen to me!" she cried over and over again. Awaking to the sound of her voice, Meg found she was twisted in a confusion of bedsheets. Still sobbing, she wrapped her arms tightly around herself and rocked slowly back and forth for many minutes.

Meg glanced around the sumptuous room, eased from her nightmare by the surroundings. If she must be twisted in bedsheets, they might as well be of the finest Egyptian cotton. It was not an auspicious beginning to the week, but Meg was resolved to make the most of her opportunity for success. And she intended to enjoy the process.

The Warrens wanted only the best, and since they regarded Meg as fitting into that category, they treated her to the best too. She felt like Cinderella at the ball. If the plane had been her magic pumpkin, then the Helmsley was her palace.

After showering in the pink marble bathroom, Meg shrugged into a thick terry robe provided by the hotel, grabbed a towel for her hair from a heated rack, and then called room service. Soon afterwards, her cappuccino and fresh strawberries and cream arrived. She ate her breakfast, savoring the luxury of it, then donned a cream-colored cashmere dress, tied a fine wool paisley scarf in complimentary colors around her shoulders, and gave her hair a last brushing. She was ready and waiting impatiently when her clients' limo arrived to pick her up.

It wasn't Meg's first limousine ride, of course. L.A. was

literally crawling with them. But it was especially nice to be taken care of in this manner in New York City. As she settled back to enjoy the ride, she noticed a fresh rose in a vase. Meg supposed she would have appreciated the touch if it hadn't reminded her of another rose so recently given her and discarded.

Meg stood in the foyer of the town house, waiting for Catalina Warren to make her appearance. A shiver of excitement and just a touch of fear ran through her. She had been in many fine homes in Beverly Hills, but this was the first time she had ever seen a New York town house beyond the pages of *Architectural Digest*. As Meg waited, she took a quick survey of the lavish appointments. A round, gold-leaf Louis XVI table held a large floral arrangement of cymbidium and cattleya orchids in shades of pink, mixed with lush stargazer lilies and green-streaked callas. Overhead hung a heavy crystal chandelier. As a whimsical touch, the Warrens' designer had placed a contemporary, oversize jade and ivory chess set on the marble checkerboard floor, and strewn satin damask and gold-braid pillows about as if to invite the visitor for a game.

"Welcome to New York, my dear." Catalina Warren entered wearing a pale shrimp-colored crepe Armani suit with a pale green silk shirt buttoned to her neck, her blond hair pulled back in a chignon. The large jade and gold earrings and a gold Cartier watch seemed almost casual afterthoughts.

Catalina brushed Meg's cheek with a kiss. "Did you have a good flight? Did Jeffrey treat you all right?"

"Oh yes, Mrs. Warren. It was kind of you to provide the plane. I very much appreciate your thoughtfulness. As a result, I'm rested and ready to get to work. Please, do show me this wonderful space I've been hearing so much about." Meg gave the woman an enthusiastic smile.

"Right this way. Do you mind climbing the stairs? We could take the elevator, but personally, I prefer to walk. It's so much better for the figure."

"I absolutely agree," Meg said, following her hostess who was already mounting the wide, curving stairway cushioned in plush rose-colored carpet. Meg wasn't surprised that the woman hadn't waited for her reply. It was the prerogative of the wealthy to assume that their wishes would be honored without question. Meg fought off the instinct to be intimidated by Catalina Warren. Although she was only slightly older than Meg, her lifetime of world travel in some of the world's wealthiest social circles had made their mark. Mrs. Warren had no need to feign sophistication; she personified it. Meg kept her poise with a silent pep talk. *Remember Meg, you have a unique service to offer and you're going to earn every dime you make on this project.*

Down a broad hall that doubled as a private art gallery and through a tall, wide door, Meg was ushered into a large, high-ceilinged room. "Wonderful!" Meg breathed as she looked around, her imagination already beginning to whir.

"It was originally used as a small ballroom, but I don't like to confine my parties to a single space. Do you think you can do anything with it?" Mrs. Warren pursed her lips ever so slightly, a tiny frown on her face, giving the impression that perhaps, after all, the space wouldn't be quite adequate.

Meg reined in her enthusiasm enough to answer, "Oh, I'm certain I can do something with it. Something wonderful. I'm looking forward to talking with Albert. As you know, I like even my youngest clients to have a say about their rooms. I hope I'll have an opportunity soon."

"Albert is in preschool this morning, but perhaps you'd like to have lunch with him? I believe he and Wendy, his nanny, are planning to ride horses in the park afterwards, so that may be your best opportunity. Oh, and Meg, I hope you've set aside Friday evening for our little party. I've invited some people with whom you might enjoy becoming acquainted. Now if you'll excuse me, I must get back to my desk. I'm sure you'll do better without my interference anyway. If you need anything, please use the intercom over there.''

"Thank you. I'm eager to get started." Meg took the measuring tape out of her briefcase and went to work, somewhat amused at the thought of five-year-old Albert squeezing her into his busy schedule. It was Meg's policy not to make judgments on her clients' lifestyles. Instead, she attempted to put herself in their place so that she could create something uniquely suited to them. Meg was always pleased when her clients remarked how closely she had matched their personalities to her designs. Vague shapes for the room took form in Meg's mind as she began the process of her newest creation.

Over a lunch of chili dogs ("They're organic, you know," Albert assured her) and skim milk, Meg questioned the little boy about his current enthusiasms. She got an earful about Ninja Turtles and Power Rangers while she reflected on the similarities between American kids of all classes. Searching for a more individual approach, Meg managed to change the subject. "Your mother tells me you've taken up riding. Do you have your own horse?"

"Yes. I have a pony. I named him Charger."

"Nice name. Does he take you charging over the prairie after buffalo, or through the desert in pursuit of camel thieves?"

"No," the little boy answered impatiently. "He takes me charging through Central Park."

"But don't you ever pretend that you and Charger are

off on some quest to save the world and best the bad guys?''

''No, I'm too grown-up for that.''

''Yes, I can see that you've changed a lot since I did your room last year in Los Angeles. Perhaps you have some ideas about what you'd like for your new playroom?''

''No, that's your job.''

''Right.'' She was definitely going to earn every penny on this job. *Too bad only rich kids get the benefit of your talent.* The thought came to Meg before she'd remembered their source. *Go away and leave me to my work, Matthew Aaberg.*

Matt caught his breath as 30,000 snow geese and 1,000 swans wheeled before the setting sun, slowly flapping their huge wings before settling on the marshes and lake for their evening rest. The beauty of the spectacle touched a chord deep within him, a oneness with nature that left him with a sense of awe and humility toward its creator. The story they were doing on the Stonylake Wild Bird Refuge was, without a doubt, going to be one of the best ever. Having begun his career as a photojournalist, Matt was excited about the striking images his cameramen were capturing. As he always did, he'd brought along his own camera to take some stills for himself and he looked forward to the results.

Matt wished Meg could be with him to share the experience, or at least to hear about it when he got home. *Home.* It had become a loaded word with him. Matt had been urging Meg to come home, but it wasn't until now that he realized that the home he had been thinking about was his. Matt didn't know if meeting Meg had triggered a nesting instinct in him, like that of the birds he was documenting, or if the timing had been coincidental. He did know that the more he resolved not to think of her, the more she invaded his thoughts, his yearning for her only intensifying.

Leave it to Rachel to set him straight on what he really wanted from Meg. Not the sort of casual relationships he'd had up till now. No. To his astonishment, it was about sharing his life with her, making a family together. Only that could satisfy. Anything less would be unthinkable.

As for Meg's needs? He hoped that hers pretty much dovetailed with his own. And thanks again to Rachel, he'd finally got it through his thick head that Meg's career was as important to her as his was to him. She deserved his respect for her accomplishments.

What was Rachel's next charge? Oh, yes . . . figure out what he had to lose or gain by the effort of winning Meg. Matt's ego had taken a lot of punishment lately. What more could he lose? If he could develop a strategy, as Rachel suggested, that would bring Meg to him this time, he'd have everything to gain. It would have to be a win-win solution for both of them.

Matt called it a wrap for the day and drove back to town with his crew. Stonyville, population twenty-eight give or take a few stray dogs and cats, was scattered on both sides of the rural highway. Its business section consisted of a grocery store/gas station/post office, a café, a few boarded-up buildings in various stages of decay, and a five-unit motel that catered mostly to guests who came to see the refuge at dawn or dusk and then hurried on to more agreeable accommodations.

Matt and the gang parked their gear at the motel and sauntered down to the café. It was their second night in town and already the menu looked depressingly familiar. They had discovered that ''Chicken-fried Steak with Gravy'' was a term loosely used to describe a cardboard-tough piece of meat smeared with canned, anemic-looking gravy, that the hamburgers had more gristle than meat, the "Catch of the Day" had been imported from Japan and was not quite thawed, and that the soda was warm and flat. He supposed it would have been funny if they weren't at the mercy of the establishment for more than one meal.

The crew hung around the restaurant for lack of anything better to do, playing the jukebox and gabbing until the place closed, at 7.00 P.M. sharp. They wandered back to the motel where they had already discovered its peculiar amenities: a tennis court without a net and a fishing pond that was so private only Ernie, the owner, seemed to have access to it. Thankfully, there was a TV in every room. Matt retired to his unit and switched on the tube, hoping for a diversion of some kind—any kind. Twiddling with the dial, he found it odd that he could get only one channel, a sitcom rerun. But hey, what could one expect way out in the sticks? Matt fluffed the pillows behind his back and stretched out on the bed, already putting his mind in neutral. Suddenly, the program switched. This time it was a game show. Matt hated game shows almost as much as Saturday morning bowling, so he got up and tried the dial again. The dial didn't move, but surprisingly, another channel switched on. This station was more to his liking, and he smiled as he turned back towards the bed. But before he could get settled, the sound on the blasted thing told him that the channel had been changed once again. This was too much.

Matt jerked open the motel door and poked out his head to try to determine what was going on. The sight before him was comical. His three men, in various stages of undress, were peering out of their doors too. Their faces, each illuminated by a porch light, revealed a full catalog of puzzlement and irritation. Matt grumbled something about seeing what the hell was going on, pulled on his boots, and stomped off to the office. Through the lighted window, the men could see the silhouette of Matt gesturing to an equally animated Ernie. Several minutes later Matt returned, shaking his head, a smile threatening to break through his grim countenance.

"Fellas, you're not going to believe this," he began, scratching his chin in his own disbelief. "Do you see that dish over there?" He pointed to a satellite dish standing off to one side of the place. They all nodded. "Well, it feeds directly into Ernie's TV. He can choose any number of over a hundred channels. The catch is that our TVs are fed off of his, so what Ernie chooses to watch, we watch. And it seems that old Ernie is into channel surfing, so we're in for a fun-filled evening of grab bag entertainment."

The night air was filled with moaning and a few random swear words.

"I suggest we all pray for the weather to hold, and that we get a good night's sleep so we can do a perfect job tomorrow. That'll get us out of here as fast as possible. Any objections?"

"Are you kidding?" came a reply.

"Won't be soon enough for me!" came another.

Matt said good night to the men and went back to his room. He propped himself up on the bed once again, and stared into space. *Here's to the glamour jobs.* Well, this would be a good time to work on his plan. He dug out his pad and pencil and began searching the archives of his brain.

Matt called up the "Meg" tape and rewound it to day one, moment one. A soft smile played on his lips as he remembered her on the plane, standing within a hair's breadth of him, trying to stuff her coat and hat into the overhead bin before sliding past him to her seat. She had been a feast for his eyes and he couldn't keep them from her. Then he remembered her face, pale and panicked.

She'd put up a certain resistance from the moment he'd stepped in to rescue her.

You don't deny you have Irish blood, do you? . . . Is your name Rose? You remind me of a long-stemmed red rose.

My name starts with "m" and ends with "g" . . . after my non-Irish grandmother.

That's a great idea. Thanks. She'd said those words as she snatched the pillow away from him. She'd left him feeling awfully foolish, but he'd been hooked.

Portland is dark, wet, and stodgy. L.A. is bright, fun, and exciting.

You don't like my company? he'd asked her.

Let's just say a little goes a long way.

Freeze-frame . . . a clue. Maybe he'd gone about winning her in all the wrong ways. True, he hadn't revealed to Meg that he was a television personality, but still, he had only let her see the glib showman, not the genuine human he knew himself to be. A wave of shame washed over him. How could he have been so stupid? He was certainly getting a lesson in humility. Matt supposed it would be a waste of time to hold a pity party. Who would come? He was tired of being alone.

Okay. So he had been incredibly brainless. What now? It seemed that the best thing to do would be to let Meg make the next move. "What does Meg want?" Rachel had asked. Matt engaged the tape again.

I'm a little tense about going home . . . I'm looking forward to seeing my niece again . . . I'm an interior designer. I love to do kids' rooms.

Freeze-frame. The clues were coming thick and fast and Matt rapidly scribbled them down. Meg had some kind of a problem with her family, but there was an obvious attachment too. If he found out what the problem was, maybe he could help straighten it out. Did Meg really hate Portland? Or was it just too close to her family? L.A. seemed to represent opportunity. Did Portland have anything to offer her?

Matthew, we're both very busy people. It's best to say good-bye now. The tape had resumed. That first kiss! Maybe it was she who'd inadvertently planted the homing device then, continuing to draw him near.

He remembered spotting her at the skating rink, her green eyes lighting up with obvious pleasure when he approached her table. The look of suppressed excitement when he'd picked her up for skiing. The magical day on the mountain. He went through it all, memory bit by memory bit. His heart began to beat a happy tattoo. *That about does it for rational thinking tonight.*

Chapter Fifteen

Meg stood among the flowering orange trees with a couple of animated women discussing children's fantasies and extolling the benefits of imagination. It was Friday evening and she was once again Cinderella, this time attending a ball in the guise of a party given by Catalina Warren and her husband, John. A *small* party, Catalina had emphasized; only about eighty people. Flying in the orange trees from California in Meg's honor was a nice touch. The caterers had carried out the California theme by serving tiny tamales, guacamole in puff pastry, and other hybrid delectables. The bar featured margaritas in a dozen flavors.

Catalina was stunning in a butterfly-yellow and emerald-green gown fashioned by La Croix, set off by an emerald and diamond choker. And, like a butterfly, she flitted from one group of guests to another, making certain everyone was enjoying themselves. John Warren, who had jetted in just in time for the festivities, appeared handsome and at ease in his tux. Meg giggled to herself, thinking that he probably had to choose which of his several tuxedos to wear, unlike the men she knew who would have had to rent theirs.

Meg had selected a crystal-pleated, sapphire-hued dress with a tulip-shaped skirt that stopped just above her knees, emphasizing her shapely hips and long legs. Its fitted bodice featured a tantalizing, low, sweetheart neckline. One side of Meg's hair was pulled back with a gold comb revealing a large pearl-drop and lapis earring. Although Meg's dress wasn't quite as elaborate as the gown the mice had created for Cinderella, she felt beautiful. Judging from admiring glances cast her way, the choice had been entirely successful.

As for Prince Charming, he hadn't shown up yet, but Meg wasn't so very anxious to meet him anyway. The last thing she needed was to be rescued. Matt had tried it, with disastrous results. If she could rewrite the story, she'd find a way for Cinderella and her Prince to be equal partners in their life's journey together. Meg sighed wistfully. If only Matt wasn't such a Neanderthal. Despite his flaws, he wasn't an easy man to forget.

The week had been a busy one. She had had to operate on faith that her design for the playroom would be acceptable to both Albert and his parents, since no hint of an idea could be extracted from any of them, nor did they have time to review her proposal. "Surprise us, Meg," Catalina had answered and waved her hand airily. Their casual attitude had taken some of the fun out of the project, but Meg was not to be deterred. She had contracted with painters, cabinetmakers, carpenters, carpet layers, electricians, floor installers, and plumbers to carry out her design, and was allotting one week in late February for all the materials to be delivered and installed. She planned to return to New

York then to supervise the operation. It was very much like staging a campaign or a war game. Everything had to fall into place at precisely the right time.

"As I was saying, I'm so anxious to see what you do with Albert's playroom. It was an absolute stroke of genius for Catalina to think of converting that old ballroom. Maybe she'll start a trend. Why, you could have more business here in New York than you can handle. How would you like that?" The woman who was speaking gave Meg's arm a patronizing pat.

Meg forced a laugh. "I think I'll just take it one step at a time and concentrate on the project at hand. Would you please excuse me?"

Meg made her escape, found the powder room, and shut the door. She stared at her image in the mirror. What she expected, she wasn't sure, but the face that looked back, although as glamorous as any woman could wish, had a sadness that even the smile she tried on couldn't dispel. *I should be elated, exhilarated. Isn't this what I've been working toward? Aren't all my dreams coming true?* The empty feeling gnawing inside of her was a rude surprise. It was as if, after years of attempting to scale a difficult mountain, fighting freezing temperatures and gale-force winds, crossing chasms and treacherous snowfields, she'd finally reached the summit, only to find the view obscured by thick, dark clouds. *It's only because I'm tired. It's been a big week.* The face in the mirror continued to stare stubbornly, unconvinced by her arguments. Meg squared her shoulders and returned to the party, grimly determined to have a good time.

Sitting in the projection room, Matt studied the segment on the wild bird refuge one last time before putting his stamp of approval on it. After a day of editing, he had the story down to six minutes: Matt interviewing a wildlife biologist who explained the effects of the recent drought, footage of a coyote intently watching the incoming birds, and the heart of the piece . . . the magnificent waterfowl, rising out of the lake at dawn and swooping back in at sunset. There was no doubt in his mind that it was one of the best films he had done, a benchmark for future work. Matt's instinct for survival had resurfaced and he was once again at the top of his form. He felt incredibly focused. Maybe, he thought to himself as he left the studio and headed his Scout towards Hazel Creek, his good mood was because, at last, he knew exactly what he wanted—Meg's heart.

Matt was uncharacteristically nervous when he called the Careys on his return from Stonylake. He had no way of knowing what Meg might have said about him, but he knew that now was not the time for timidity. To his surprise, Pam seemed pleased to hear from him and insisted he come for dinner.

Alan met Matt at the front door and shook his hand with gusto. "Come in, my boy. Good to see you again."

"Good to see you too, Alan. I sure do appreciate the dinner invitation. Sometimes I get a little tired of bachelor cooking." He gave Alan a rueful grin.

"Well, come on into the kitchen and say 'hello' to the cook," Alan invited, indicating that Matt should follow. Matt found himself in the homey old kitchen, greeting Pam and being treated like a member of the family. Their dinner began with the usual exchange of pleasantries and general conversation before Alan brought up the first real topic of the evening.

"Meg mentioned you were some kind of a TV reporter. Just what is it you do, Son?"

"Well, Sir, I'm a producer and host of a public television show called 'Naturally Oregon.' "

"Is that so? I've never seen it. Don't have much time to watch television. Is it any good?"

"Alan . . ." Pam tried to protest her husband's undiplomatic question.

Matt tipped back his head and laughed heartily. "It's all right," he said to Pam, then answered Alan's question. "I guess you'll have to be the judge of that."

"Ha! Spoken like a real man." Alan waggled his spoon at Matt. "I like your style, young fellow. You'd better tell me when you're on so I can be sure to catch you."

"Tuesday nights, eight o'clock on Channel five, and Friday afternoons at four."

"Good. Good. Say, how come Meg didn't tell us about that?" Alan shot a questioning look at his wife who silently shrugged her shoulders. He turned to Matt for an answer.

"I don't think she knows," Matt mumbled, spearing a bite of vegetable.

Alan's eyebrows tilted quizzically. "You didn't tell her?"

"Nope."

"Well, I'll be damned. Yes sir, I do like your style."

Matt winced, glad he wasn't going to have to confess all of his sins to Meg's father. "Thank you," he said, his eyes on his plate.

"I bet your parents are very proud of you, Matthew," Pam offered.

"I'm afraid neither one of them is living, Pam. They both died in a plane crash several years ago."

"Oh, I'm so sorry." Pam's voice vibrated with concern. "Do you have any other family?"

"Yes, two sisters. We're quite close."

"Aaberg, Aaberg . . . Was your dad's first name Carl?"
Alan cocked his head at Matt.

Matt nodded.

"I remember now. Carl Aaberg. Wasn't he a lawyer in
Portland? Involved in a lot of environmental issues?"

"That's right," Matt answered, pleased that his father's
memory still lived on. "The crash happened while he and
Mom were inspecting a stand of old-growth forest that was
being clear-cut."

"Yeah. I remember his name being in the paper from
time to time, don't you Pam? So, you chose to pick up
where your old man left off?" Alan went on, not waiting
for his wife's answer.

"Well, not exactly," Matt said slowly. "I believe in the
causes he fought for, but I have to support them in my own
way. Dad wanted me to be an attorney like himself, but
I'm much better as a reporter. My dad's job was to persuade people; my job is to educate people."

"Makes sense."

"This meal is delicious, Pam. I really appreciate your
inviting me."

"Well, I was wrong about another friend of Meg's once.
I just wanted to see if perhaps this time I was right." Pam
looked directly at Matt as she spoke, lifting her chin ever
so slightly.

Matt smiled to himself, remembering where else he'd
seen that gesture. "I appreciate your frankness." He nodded his approval. "I hope I pass, because I'm planning on
being around for a long while."

"Be a good trick, what with Meg living down in L.A.
and you here in Portland," Alan snorted.

Matt took a deep breath before answering. "That's why
I wanted to talk with you. I have a plan to change that, but

before I put it in motion, I need to know how you both feel about Meg moving back here.''

"Why, that would be wonderful, wouldn't it Alan?" Pam clasped her hands.

"You betcha! But how are you going to get her to do that, Son?"

"Meg told me Los Angeles has all kinds of opportunities for her career. She also told me that she'd love to do more work for less fortunate children. When I read in *The Oregonian* that Children's Hospital is planning an addition, I got to thinking that Portland just might have what she's looking for. I recognized the name of the architectural firm that got the contract. One of the principals was a friend of my father's and . . .'' Matt continued to lay out his plan, interspersed with suggestions and encouragement from Pam and Alan. When he had finished, Alan spoke up.

"That sounds like a real fine scheme, Matthew. When will you be putting it into motion?"

Matt rubbed his chin thoughtfully. "Well, actually, I've told you the easy part. There's a little problem that I really need your help with, Alan."

"Shoot."

Matt plunged forward. "You may not know it, but I visited Meg a couple of weeks ago in L.A. The last thing she said to me was, 'You're just like my father, always thinking that he knows what's best for me.' And then she told me she never wanted to see me again."

"Oh dear," Pam murmured.

Alan made a choking sound, then began to cough spastically, tears rolling down his cheeks. Pam got up to get something for him from the kitchen while Matt pounded him on the back. When the fit had subsided, Matt spoke.

"Sorry, sir. I know it's upsetting, but I think we have to deal with it."

"What makes you think Meg has a real beef?" Alan rasped out, mopping at the tears with his napkin.

"Well, sir, I talked it over with my sister, and she helped me see my error."

"Which was . . . ?"

"Not only did I want to star in Meg's life, I was trying to be her producer and director. Meg is a very competent person. She can take care of herself, and I didn't acknowledge that. If things are ever going to be good between us, I've got to appreciate her for who she is, not try to change her."

Pam, about to return with a glass of water, overheard the conversation and paused to listen.

"And you think I'm guilty of that too?" Alan's eyes sparked with challenge.

"Are you?" Matt could feel his adrenaline pumping. So much depended on how Meg's father would react. Both men were silent for several moments before Alan spoke again, his stare never wavering.

"You've got a lot of nerve bringing it up."

"Yes, Sir." Matt returned his look.

"I've done my best by Meg and her brother, by God," Alan said loudly. "My own parents had nothing. I had to do everything the hard way, but I made a success of myself. I gave my kids a leg up, helped put them through college, tried to give them a little counsel along the way. But Meg . . ." Alan snorted. "Meg doesn't want my advice. She thinks she already knows it all!"

"Or maybe she wants to do things her own way, just like you did."

Alan squinted his eyes in speculation. "You think that's it?"

"Maybe. Why don't you ask her?"

"I . . . We've never talked like that. I wouldn't know how to do it." For the first time since the conversation began, Alan sounded uncertain.

"It'd be risky, all right."

The older man inhaled loudly, his shoulders rising, then slowly exhaled just as loudly. Matt held his own breath, wondering what was coming. "Risky, huh? Well, I didn't get to where I am without taking a few gambles."

"That's what I figured." Matt released a silent sigh of relief.

Alan straightened. "Let's see about dessert. Pam," he called loudly, "have we got any dessert for this young fellow?"

"Coming right up!" Pam answered so quickly that Matt wondered if she had been eavesdropping.

"Say, Matthew," Alan spoke in a low, confidential voice as he escorted him to the door at the end of the evening, "just why are you so fired up about getting Meg to move back here?"

Matthew grinned. "Guess you want to know what my intentions are toward your daughter, right?"

"Right." Alan gave Matt an answering grin.

Matt's face grew serious. "I love her, Alan. And I hope to marry her someday." He said it with quiet confidence. Saying it aloud for the first time felt good . . . so good.

"I see. And you're willing to change if it'll make a difference to her?"

"I'm making some changes because I should. I can only hope that Meg approves."

"Good for you, Son. Pam and I will try to do our part,

too. Maybe we'll all get lucky." Alan clapped Matt on the shoulder.

"Maybe we will. Now remember, we don't want Meg to know we're behind this thing. If she gets wind of our involvement, she's likely to reject it out of hand. Here's my business card. You can call me at the station or . . ." Matt scribbled a number on the back of the card before handing it to Alan, "at my apartment. Thanks for a great dinner, Pam," he called in her direction. Matt extended his hand to Alan. "Thanks, again."

Alan thoughtfully watched Matt walk towards his truck. He called after him. "Hey, I'm looking forward to catching you on the tube Tuesday night, and don't be a stranger around here, all right?"

"Thank you! Good night."

Pam had suggested that they involve Rosalind in the plan. She would be able to provide a résumé and portfolio of Meg's work to Porter, Macadam, and Hawthorn, Architects. She might also be able to encourage Meg to take the position. Matt called Rosalind and carefully laid the strategy out for her, explaining its benefits in precise order. First, he described a job that appeared to be perfectly suited to Meg—working with a respected architectural firm primarily in the field of pediatric interiors. Rosalind listened, but clearly was not swayed. However, by the time Matt finished with his second point—that Meg's father was more willing to accept his daughter's independent ways—Rosalind was forced to admit that he had a strong case. Then Matt confessed his own motives for wanting Meg back in Oregon. "I really care for Meg and I'm hoping I can redeem myself."

"Matt, it seems to me that the possibility of you making up with Meg is about as good as a snowball's chance in hell. Besides, I don't think you realize what you're asking. Maybe moving back to Oregon is in Meg's best interest, but it's certainly not in mine! She's my best friend.''

''Yes, I know, and I'm sorry to put you in such a bind, but we really need your help.''

''What makes you think I can be of any use? You know how stubborn Meg is.''

''Don't I ever. Look, it might not work, but we've got to try. If there's anything I can do in return for you, I'd be glad to.'' Matt silently willed Rosalind to cooperate.

''It's not likely you can find me another best friend.''

''You're right about that.'' *Say ''Yes,'' Rosalind.*

''All right, all right, I'll do it. But I can't promise you the results you want. Meg has been awfully quiet since she came back from New York. I'm really not in touch with what she's thinking right now.''

''The decision will be Meg's, of course. I just want to give her some options. I really appreciate your assistance.''

The phone call Meg had received was a surprise to say the least. A job offer in Portland was just about the last thing she'd expected. Even though she told herself she wasn't interested, she had an unsettled feeling about it. She sought Rosalind, suggesting a game of racquetball. Afterward, she approached her with the problem. ''Can I talk with you for a minute?''

''Sure. What's up?''

''Well, I got a call—it came right out of the blue—from an architectural firm in Portland asking if I'd like to go up there for an interview. Their spokeswoman said they were impressed with my work and needed someone of my caliber in their pediatric interior design department. I was absolutely floored; I don't even know how they heard of me. I told them 'Thanks, but no thanks,' of course.'' Meg gave a little laugh.

'' 'Of course'?'' Rosalind didn't look amused.

"Of course! There's no way I'm moving back to Oregon!''

"Why not?''

"You know why not. I can't stand it there. It's too restrictive. There aren't any opportunities for me.''

"But you've just told me about a position that sounds wonderful, right up your alley.''

"All right,'' Meg admitted, "it's also too close to my parents. You know I don't get along with them all that well.''

"Didn't you tell me that you and your mom had a good heart-to-heart at Christmas?''

"Yes, but things are just as bad as ever with Dad.''

"Maybe you ought to try a little harder. You might be pleasantly surprised.''

"Look, I don't want to argue about this; I've already made up my mind. I just wanted you to tell me I did the right thing.'' Meg searched her friend's face for a hint of understanding.

Rosalind frowned stubbornly at her. "You came to the wrong person if that's what you want. You're my best friend, Meg, but I don't mind telling you, I think you're making a big mistake. At least go for the interview. What can that hurt?''

"It's obvious you don't understand. I'm sorry I ever brought up the subject.'' Meg got up to leave.

Rosalind got up too, her face flushed. "It's you who doesn't understand, Meg. Why, I'd give anything for a job like that and a chance to be a near a family that loves me as much as your family obviously loves you. In fact, you know what I'm going to do? Since you don't want it, I'm going to apply for that job. I've had enough of L.A.''

"You're not serious!"

"I certainly am!" Rosalind grabbed up her gym bag and ran off. Meg shook her head in bewilderment, wondering what had come over her usually agreeable friend.

Chapter Sixteen

The call came when Matt was having his weekly dinner at the Careys'. Matt had taken Alan at his word and had made a habit of dining with them. Even if they hadn't been Meg's parents, he would have enjoyed their down-home hospitality and easy manner. Alan never said another word to Matt about the conversation they'd had that first evening concerning his attitude toward his daughter. Matt knew that he wasn't the kind of man to talk about such things, but he was pretty sure Alan had taken his words to heart.

Pam got up to answer the phone, then came back into the dining room. "It's for you, Matt. It's Rosalind." Matt went into the kitchen and picked up the receiver.

"Hi, Rosalind. How's it going?"

"Not too good, Matthew. I'm sorry, I really tried, but I just couldn't talk Meg into taking the job. I couldn't even get her to go for an interview." Matt could hear the frustration in her voice.

153

Matt slammed his fist on the countertop. "Damn, I wish I could talk to her, but there's no way she'd listen to me."

"I know how disappointed you must be."

"I guess I should have known better, but I had to try. Maybe I'll be able to think of something else." Matt rubbed his chin absently.

"Matt, I'm not sure how to break this to you. I blew up at Meg for being so stubborn and told her that I was going to try for the job. Then I realized I really meant it, so I called and got an interview for myself. I hope you and Pam and Alan understand."

Matthew felt as if he had been hit by a California earthquake. When he caught his breath, he told her, "I guess I can't blame you. It's not your fault Meg doesn't want it."

"I was hoping you'd say that. It's just that ever since I broke up with my boyfriend, I've felt as if I've needed some sort of a change. Maybe this is it. I like Portland, I love Pam and Alan, and the job seems a good fit."

Matt relaxed a bit. "Hey, I'll be happy for you if it works out. In fact, I'll introduce you around if you decide to move here."

"That's really great of you. Maybe there's another way to get through to Meg. Don't give up yet. Please give my regards to Pam and Alan and tell them I'm sorry."

Matt returned to the dining room to see Pam blinking back tears and Alan holding her hand, trying to comfort her. The look on his face wasn't much happier. "I guess you heard. Meg's not interested," Matt said, sinking into his chair with a sigh. "I'm sorry I got your hopes up."

"Matt, you had to give it a shot. We don't blame you for anything," Alan assured him.

"There's something else you should know. Rosalind's decided to try for the job. She says she hopes you understand."

"Well, I'll be!" exclaimed Alan.

Pam was quiet for a moment, considering the new development. "Of course we understand. That would be very nice. Rosalind's almost like a daughter to us, and at least Meg might want to visit more often. I'm going to call her right back and insist that she stay with us while she's up here for her interview."

Rosalind caught Meg as she was picking up her mail. She chatted excitedly as they entered Meg's apartment. "This is great—your having me for dinner and taking me to the airport. The traffic ought to have cleared by the time we're ready to leave."

"I'm happy to do it. Besides, it's important not to be rushed before a flight," Meg said as she looked over the mail—a couple of catalogs, one bill, and a homemade valentine from Eliza Jane. "Okay. Let's see what's in the package." Meg got out a knife and began cutting the wrapping tape. She removed an object wrapped in tissue and unwrapped it to reveal a slightly battered tin in the shape of a log cabin.

"Look at this, Rosalind. It's an old maple syrup can." Meg held it for inspection.

"Isn't that darling. Who sent it?"

"Here's a card. All it says is 'Happy Valentine's Day.' " Meg had a strong suspicion she already knew. She removed the remaining tissue.

"Is that all? No signature or anything?"

"Nothing else. There isn't even a return address."

"What's the postmark?"

Meg looked at the label again. "Portland," she said, her suspicions confirmed.

"Is it from your mother?"

Meg continued her pretense. "I don't think so, especially without a note."

"Does it say anything on the can?" Rosalind persisted.

Meg picked it up and turned it around. A slight sound inside caught her attention. "It's got something in it." She shook the can near her ear. "It sounds like pebbles. Let's see . . ." Meg unscrewed the lid on the chimney and turned the cabin upside down as she held out her palm to catch whatever might spill out. Into her hand plopped two candies, each with an *M* on it. Meg put the can down on the counter and studied them. One was brown, the other red.

Rosalind had been watching the procedure with interest. "Is that all that's in there? Whoever sent it was sure cheap!"

Meg laughed dryly. "I believe it's a little joke, Rosalind."

"I don't get it."

"Actually, I don't either. It doesn't really matter." Meg shrugged her shoulders, doing her best to sound unconcerned. She walked to the refrigerator. "Let's heat up our food and eat."

Returning to her apartment after taking Rosalind to the airport, Meg went straight to the kitchen and picked up the little tin cabin and the candies. Taking them into the dining room, she placed them carefully on the table, then sat down to think. Absently, she moved the two candies around in her hand while she remembered the time at the beach when Matt had solemnly sorted out all the tan and red ones and given them to her. It had been too deliberate not to have some sort of significance.

This hadn't been the first gift he'd sent her since they parted. A couple of weeks earlier, she'd received a photograph he had taken of her with one arm draped around Snowwoman. It had torn at her already bloodied heart, but for reasons she couldn't explain, Meg hadn't been able to throw it out the way she had the rose. Instead, she tucked the photo deep in a dresser drawer.

And now this. The little log cabin surely stood for the one Matt had taken her to that beautiful, awful night. Breaking the code of the candies was harder. Meg fingered them, trying to decipher their meaning. They were smooth and round. They had a sweet taste. There were two of them, one brown and one red. Each had the letter *M* on it. They had been inside the cabin. A smile began to spread across Meg's face as the meaning dawned on her. She and Matt had been in the cabin . . . just the two of them. Matt and Meg. M and M. Red hair and brown. Meg put *persistent* and *clever* at the top of her list, and added *romantic*.

Meg's smile faded and her hand clenched around the candies as she pondered his reason for sending the gift. Technically, at least, he had honored her wishes about never seeing her again, but he was making darn sure that she wasn't going to forget him. As if she ever could. He probably was hoping that she would call him and say something like, ''Oh Matthew, that was a darling gift. How sweet you are. All is forgiven.'' Fat chance! There was nothing he could do now to change her mind. Just as there was nothing she could do to forget him.

She knew if she wrote and asked him to quit all forms of communication with her, he would oblige. That would guarantee she'd lose him forever.

''Darn!'' she shouted, pounding the table with both fists. ''Darn! Darn! Darn!'' She continued to beat on the table causing the log cabin to dance up and down with a clatter. Hot tears rushed down her cheeks. Meg was infuriated with Matt for being so cavalier with her feelings, mad at herself for caring that he was. Her anger expanded, and she gave in to the irrational thoughts she had been holding at bay all week. How dare Rosalind go off to Portland, taking the job that was meant for her? Claiming her family's affection? And why did her New York project leave a bad taste in her mouth every time she thought of it? Meg cried and pounded, pounded and cried. Eventually the storm waned, and she buried her face in her arms, sobbing softly. Presently, she lifted her head, unclenched her fists, and stared through swollen eyes at the melted mess in her hand.

Chapter Seventeen

Wandering through the litter of wood and the tangle of wires, over drop cloths and under scaffolding, Meg waited for the workers and delivery vans to arrive. Two more days and her New York project would be finished. The Warrens had arranged to be in California during the remodeling, so Meg was staying at the town house with a skeleton staff.

Her evenings had been much different than she had expected. She managed to see a Broadway show, but otherwise did not venture out. Instead, Meg snuggled in front of the television and knitted on a throw she had started for herself months ago. When there was nothing good to watch, she sat and knitted and thought.

Meg could certainly chalk up the daytimes as one big learning experience. Her first lesson was adjusting to the habits of the workmen in this high-charged city. Not one of them had yet shown up on time. At first Meg had been upset, but she came to expect the standard catalog of excuses that often had to do with the traffic on the bridges, or the difficulty of getting the equipment up from the street, or a fight with the wife. Lunch took a full hour, of course. And then everyone went home at 3:00 P.M. to escape the late-afternoon traffic. Meg was infinitely glad that she had extended the project to two weeks. It was going to be close, but it looked as if the room might be completed in time for Catalina and Albert's return.

Although the craftsmen had short days, when they actually worked, the results were superior. The small powder room was almost complete, the design of the tile echoing the theme of the playroom. The framing in the large room had all been constructed, drywalled, taped, and mostly painted. The trompe l'oeil artists had directed their magic wands at the wooden floor.

The intercom's buzz interrupted Meg's thoughts. "You have a delivery, Miss Carey," came a voice.

"I'll be right there." Meg hurried out to the elevator. In the lobby, she greeted the delivery man, noticing with a frown that the snowfall, which had begun in the early hours of the morning, had grown in ferocity. She directed the man to the freight elevator and stood watching as the workers began unloading large wooden forms and wrestling them through the door of the elevator. Meg had heard horror stories of designers having to hoist grand pianos through upper apartment windows, and she had been careful to avoid a similar scenario on her own project. Still, it was a relief to see everything fitting as she had planned.

Meg peered outside, watching two of the men unload the last piece. To her horror, one of the men tripped on the curb and went sprawling into the gutter. His end of the object followed his trajectory and landed in the ooze next to him. The man recovered, picked his burden back up and proceeded through the door and past Meg. She moaned when she saw its condition. The paint was stained with snow and grime, and it was dripping copious amounts of water. One corner was badly chipped. Meg called for furniture pads and twine and directed the men to wrap the piece up as best they could so that Catalina's carpets would not be ruined. Then she propped herself up against the nearest wall, closed her eyes, and practiced the breathing exercises Matt had taught her. When she was finished, she took the elevator back up, marched purposely into the playroom, made a complete survey of the damage and put in some important phone calls. She had no idea how the artisans would respond to her pleas for help, only that if they didn't, she could kiss her New York reputation good-bye.

"Your realm, m'Lord!" Meg held a long, shiny trumpet to her lips and blew a note, then bowed with a flourish before the gaping Albert, his mother, and Albert's nanny, standing on the floor painted to look like ancient paving stones. The little group had arrived minutes after Meg's cleaning crew had flicked the last pieces of plaster and dust from the room. It had only been the day before that Meg had been able to persuade her artisans to make an emergency repair to the fallen artwork after drying it out with a giant heater fan.

"Albert, don't you have anything to say?" Catalina asked her son. For once, the little boy seemed at a loss for words as they all stood gazing at "Albert's Kingdom," as Meg had dubbed it. In the foreground was a moat lined with a blue beanbag river and crossed by two bridges—one, a swaying wooden ramp—both balanced on upper and lower cables. Overhead hand grips strung on a chain comprised a third means of crossing. On the other side of the moat stood the castle, which boasted a tall, round tower crowned by a parapet casting a shadow of its cutout shape on the ceiling. A pulley jutted out from a high wall, ready to lower a bucket for supplies. A large stuffed dragon looked benevolently down on them from his perch on top of a slide that ended in the moat. Scaling one side of the castle was a rope ladder. Coats of arms proudly adorned the walls that were painted to look like stone building blocks, and banners fluttered everywhere in the slight breeze created by cleverly concealed fans. Strategically placed lighting gave the scene a mystical appearance.

Meg had to admit it took her breath away when she stood back to look at it. She had designed it with the twin goals of providing physical activity and a stimulant for imagination. But would Albert, with his privileged upbringing, appreciate it? Meg waited in suspense for his response.

"Perhaps you should explore," suggested Wendy, handing Albert the hobbyhorse that Meg had had crafted to look like his real horse.

Albert suddenly came to life. "All right!" he yelled, and galloped excitedly toward the bridge. Meg felt a surge of relief.

"Well Meg, it seems that you've got a success on your hands," Catalina observed. "Congratulations!" She leaned over with a warm smile and gave Meg a little hug.

"Thank you, Catalina. I'm pleased that Albert likes it and I'm glad I had the opportunity to do it. I want to have the room photographed, as stipulated in our contract. I'll be contacting you about that soon."

"Yes, of course. I'm certain there will be more than one magazine that's interested in featuring it."

Meg nodded. "I've had a couple of nibbles already. Now, if you'll excuse me, I believe Jeffrey is waiting at the airport."

"Good-bye, my dear. I hope we'll see you again soon."

* * *

Meg entered her apartment several hours later, exhausted from the flight and the events of the last weeks. Her plan was to get some rest, then call her parents. She'd had a lot of time to think. She bridled at the implication the estrangement with her father was her fault, but she realized that she should at least try to talk with him about it in person as soon as she could get away. Anything would be better than continuing her unsuccessful evasion of the conflict. She couldn't count on her father changing; she was going to have to accept him for who he was, just as she hoped that someday, he would do the same for her. She admitted that a good relationship with her parents was important—at least as important as a fancy job in New York City.

Meg threw down her bags and punched the rewind button on her answering machine. Invitations from casual friends, routine messages, and then, toward the end, Rosalind's voice. "Meg, I don't care what time it is when you get this message, please call me right away. It's urgent!"

Meg let the machine run on, hoping for an additional clue as to the nature of the emergency. A few more routine calls and it stopped. Impatiently, Meg dialed Rosalind's number. She hadn't seen much of her friend since Rosalind's return from her Portland interview, and the subsequent news that she had been offered the job and accepted. On the pretense of preparing for her New York project, Meg had pretty much kept her distance. She wondered if the crisis had anything to do with her friend's impending move.

"Hello," Rosalind answered the phone on the first ring.

"Rosalind, this is Meg. I just got in and heard your message. Is something wrong?"

"Meg, are you sitting down?"

"Rosalind, tell me, what is it!"

"Meg, your sister-in-law called about five hours ago.

Your father had a heart attack and is in the hospital. They've got him stabilized, so that's the good news.''

"Oh, Lord!" Meg grabbed her middle, feeling as if someone had just punched her.

"I haven't heard anything else. Chrisy called me when she couldn't get in touch with you. She said she'd call again when she gets some more news from Sean. He left for Portland as soon as he got word.''

"I have to get to the airport. I've got to go home!''

"I already have the schedule for you. The first flight that you can make leaves at five past twelve tonight. I'll call for a reservation, then I'll be right over. Now, I want you to take a good, hot shower and get into some fresh clothes. Will you do that?''

"Yes, but please hurry!''

"I'll be there shortly. Just try to keep calm.''

Oh, please God. Don't let him die. It's been so long since I told him I love him. Don't let him go now. Meg prayed fervently as she winged her way toward Portland, wondering how jet travel could seem so slow. She kept playing the dining room argument with him over and over in her head. His smile, warm and open, then slowly crumbling into ashes. It tore at her heart. He had been wrong, but she had been cruel. Then she recalled her conversation with her mother, directly afterward. *You've got your horns locked . . . you've both already lost.* Meg prayed that it wasn't too late to mend their relationship. She asked God for forgiveness and she thanked Him for her friend Rosalind, there for her when Meg needed her. Besides arranging for her flight and taking Meg to the airport, Rosalind assured her that she would take care of her clients during Meg's absence. Apparently she had thought of everything, because when Meg got off the plane, Sean was there to greet her.

"Hi, Sis," he said, throwing his arms around her and hugging her tightly.

"Is he ... is he going to be all right?" Meg's muffled question came from the depths of Sean's heavy coat.

"The doctors say he has a good chance of making it. It looks as if he'll be having a bypass, but they say the outlook is hopeful. They'll be doing some tests first thing in the morning."

"Thank God! Oh Sean, I was so scared. I kept thinking that I just wanted to tell him I love him. Can I see him now?"

"They've got him sedated. Mom's still at the hospital. I want you to take her home and let her get a little sleep. You can see him a little later in the morning. I'll stay and call you if there's any change."

"How is Mom doing?" Meg asked him as they headed towards Sean's car. It was good to be walking side by side with him, his arm around her.

Sean frowned slightly. "Mom is very calm. It's almost eerie. Kind of like she saw it coming."

"I wonder if she did. She seemed ... oh, I don't know ... different at Christmas, too. I used to think I knew everything about her, but I wonder if I really do."

Despite Meg's best efforts to stay awake, she fell asleep in her father's chair by the phone after seeing her mother off to bed. The next thing she was aware of was Pam's gentle kiss on her forehead. "Good morning, Dear. You really shouldn't sleep like that. It's bad for your spine."

"Mother! How are you feeling?"

"Your father is going to be all right. I'm going to be all right."

Meg got up and hugged her. "I'll fix us just a bite of breakfast and then we'll go back to the hospital."

At the hospital, Meg was allowed only a few minutes to

see her father. When she entered his room, he was resting. She looked at his pale face and closed eyelids, the tubes and probes coming from his body. Quietly she walked over to his bed, gently squeezed his hand, and murmured, "I love you, Dad," in his ear.

He opened his eyes in surprise, then realizing who she was, smiled weakly at her. "I love you too, Sugar. Thanks for coming."

"The doctors say you're due for a little surgery. They say if you behave yourself, you'll be fine. Think you can do that?" Meg allowed her mouth to turn up at the corners so he could see that she was teasing.

"I don't know. I'm not used to taking orders," he said, half seriously.

"No, the Careys aren't very good at that, are we?" Meg laughed, then turned serious. "I have to leave now so Sean and Mother can come in, but I'll be back soon."

"Are you all going to gang up on me? Make me behave?" he asked petulantly.

"That's about the size of it. We've got you outnumbered."

"Shucks. Guess I'll have to go along with you on this one."

"About time. Well, I'll see you later." Meg bent and kissed him.

Chapter Eighteen

They waited a lifetime, or so it seemed, for the doctor to tell them how Alan's operation had gone. At last Dr. Wagner entered the waiting room, and Meg, Pam, and Sean each desperately searched his face for a clue.

"It went very well," he assured them. "Alan is in good general shape, so he should have a successful recovery. We'll know more in the next few days, but I'm optimistic about his chances. That is, of course, if he's careful about his diet and exercise, and he takes steps to relieve the stress he's put himself under for so many years." They gave their heartfelt thanks to the surgeon and took turns hugging one another, tears of relief shining in their eyes.

Two days had elapsed since her father's surgery. Sean had gone back to work, and Meg and Pam spent their time traveling back and forth to the hospital to visit him.

"Hi, Pop. How are you doing?" Meg poked her head into his room.

"Pretty fair. Come on in."

"Are they treating you okay around here?" Meg asked as she seated herself next to the bed.

"Well, the nurses are awfully bossy, but I'm working on that."

"I'll bet you are," Meg chortled.

"I'm sure glad you're here. Is it okay, you being gone from work just now?"

"Yes, thanks to Rosalind. She's covering for me. Luckily, I just finished with the New York project."

"Say, how'd that turn out?" he said. Meg was surprised to hear a note of interest in his voice.

"Just fine. My clients seemed pleased with it."

"I'll bet you did a bang-up job, Sugar."

"Thanks, Dad."

Alan's face grew serious. "I guess I haven't been very good at telling you how proud I am of you."

"It's okay, Dad. It doesn't matter." Meg reached over to hold his hand.

"That's where you're wrong. It does matter."

"Don't worry yourself about it. You need to concentrate on getting better." Meg withdrew her hand, feeling decidedly uncomfortable. She wasn't accustomed to her father talking like this.

"No, I want to discuss it now. There are some things I need to tell you. Things like, 'I love you,' and 'I'm glad you're my daughter.' I used to think I was saying those things when I gave you advice. I guess I figured that you knew what I really meant. Hey . . ." he paused at the sight of the tears that were streaking Meg's cheeks. "I didn't mean to make you cry!"

"I know, Dad," Meg sniffled. "It's just that you never

seemed to be satisfied with who I was. What Sean did was always more important to you, especially when he got married. It seemed like getting married was a measure of his success, or adulthood, or something. I love Sean a lot, but I really got sick of it! You never seemed to be pleased with what I was doing.''

''I can see that I have some explaining to do,'' Alan said thoughtfully, a pained expression on his face. ''When your mother and I found out that they were planning to marry so young, we were terribly upset. All our hopes and dreams for Sean seemed to vanish overnight. I never would have wished the burden of a family on him at age twenty. But we had to make the best of it, didn't we? So Pam and I made a pact. We agreed we would only talk about the good things that could come out of the situation. I guess we never stopped to consider what it might mean to you.''

''I always thought you were disappointed in me because I wasn't like him.'' Meg bit her lip to halt the tears.

''Never! I've always been proud of you, my beautiful, independent daughter! In fact, I'd like to think you take after me.'' Alan grinned at her.

''Oh, Daddy!'' Meg leaned over his bed, laughing through her tears, and hugged him as best she could. She imagined she could feel the hardness in a corner of her heart dissolving into nothingness.

Later that evening, Meg called Rosalind.

''Hi, Meg,'' Rosalind answered. ''How's Alan?''

''He's coming along just fine. How are you holding up?''

''Things are all right here. I haven't taken on any new clients, so I've had the time to handle yours. I told Madeline today that I'll be leaving.''

''How did she take it?'' Meg asked.

''She said she wished me only the best.''

''Good, I'm glad. The thought of you living up here sure

seems strange. In fact, everywhere I turn these days, people are making changes. You moving up here. Chrisy going back to school. And you know what else? Mom and Dad are talking about taking an early retirement, selling the house, and spending some time traveling. I don't know if I can handle it all at once.'' Meg gave a mighty sigh.

''Brace yourself. You've got another surprise coming. Can you keep a secret?''

Meg closed her eyes, trying to prepare herself for Rosalind's news. ''I suppose I'm as ready as I'll ever be. What is it?''

Rosalind laughed. ''I think you can cope with this one. After all, Phillip says you're partly responsible.''

''Phillip? What's he up to?''

''He's going back to college next fall. He decided to follow your advice and get a degree in counseling.''

''Well, isn't that something! He'll be good. You know, Rosalind, I always thought a person should set a goal and never waver until it was accomplished, but I'm beginning to see that it's good to reevaluate one's direction from time to time. Take me, for instance. Up until now, I've been so focused on becoming a top designer, I haven't stopped to consider what else I want out of life.''

''Is there more?'' Rosalind teased.

Meg laughed. ''I did a lot of thinking while I was in New York. I've come to the conclusion that I want more of a balance in my life. For one thing, I'd like to be closer to my family.''

''Does this mean that you're getting along a little better with your father now?''

''Yes. We had a good talk and cleared up some misunderstandings. I suppose he'll always be tempted to tell me how to do things, but now I know that he really does believe in me.''

"Meg, that's great! I'm so glad."

"Anyway, I don't want you to tell anyone yet, but I've decided to look for a job in Portland after all. I'm going to try to get a couple of interviews while I'm here."

"Why don't you try Porter, Macadam, and Hawthorn?"

"No, you got the plum there. I'd be kicking myself all the time for not following through on that one. I don't know what else is out there, but I'm sure I'll eventually find something," Meg hastened to reassure her friend, hoping against hope that she was right.

"What if I told you that PM&H has been looking for two designers in their pediatric interiors department?"

"You're kidding. You're not!" Meg shrieked. "I was sure I'd blown my chance. Maybe we can still work together. Wouldn't that be wonderful?" She felt like jumping up and down like Eliza Jane did when she was excited.

"Yes, it would! I just know they'll want you."

The next morning, Meg called the architectural firm to arrange an interview. They seemed pleased to hear from her and set one up for the following day. Meg left her mother at the hospital, saying she had to do some shopping. It was all she could do to keep from confiding in Pam, but she didn't want to set her up for any more disappointments.

It had been five days since Meg's arrival, and Alan's recovery was going well. He had become quite a pet with the nurses. Meg caught him munching on a Popsicle as she entered his room.

"Aha! Just who did you bribe to get that? And I suppose it's your favorite," Meg accused him.

"Banana, and what makes you think I had to use a bribe? All it took was a little Irish charm." He winked at her.

Meg shook her head. "Dad, I just don't know what we're going to do with you."

"Take me home and love me, I guess."

"Now there's a thought. Has the doctor said anything about when they're going to spring you?"

"Day after tomorrow," Alan crowed.

"That's wonderful. Mom will sure be glad to hear it. Sean will be coming up for the weekend. I wish I could be around Sunday, but I'm going to have to leave tomorrow night. I've got to get back to work before they decide I've gone AWOL."

"I'll be sorry to see you go, but I know that keeping that job of yours is important."

"Pays the bills." She smiled, knowing that he understood.

"Enough of this," Alan said brusquely. "I've got a TV show to catch."

"I never thought I'd see my Dad become a couch potato."

"Since Christmas I've gotten addicted to a certain show on PBO. Would you like to watch it with me?"

"Sure, Dad." Meg settled back in her chair.

Alan flicked the remote and the image of a thousand wheeling snow geese filled the screen. Then the host came on, his amber-colored hair glinting in the sunlight. He was squinting slightly, but Meg knew the color of his eyes was a golden-brown. "In this segment of "Naturally Oregon," we'll take you on a trip to Stonylake Wild Bird Refuge and find out what scientists are doing to counter the effects of a recent drought."

Meg inclined her head towards the TV, her eyes fastened on the man who had haunted her for so many days and nights. She tore her gaze away and turned toward her father, bursting with questions. He shook his head at her and put his finger to his lips. She opened her mouth to ask anyway, but Alan frowned her down. Conflicting emotions clashed inside her as she watched, mesmerized, for the next thirty minutes. The man was as compelling as ever. And certainly intelligent. Matt knew just how to present the story without appearing to take sides, but Meg could feel herself and, she guessed, most of his audience, rooting for the wildlife. A surge of pride in him and his love for his subject welled up inside her. No wonder Matt had had difficulty understanding her insistence on remaining in L.A.

"My gosh! He's the producer too," Meg uttered in surprise when the credits began to roll. She glanced at her father, who had a cat-that-swallowed-the-canary kind of grin on his face. "All right, Dad. What gives?" she demanded. "How did you find out about Matt's show?"

"He told me," he said mildly.

"He told you."

"Yup."

"He just called you up one day and said, 'By the way, be sure to catch my show on Channel five'?"

"Not exactly."

"What, exactly?" Meg demanded.

"We've become friends. I like the guy," Alan replied.

"Oh, brother. It's worse than I feared. What else haven't you told me?" Meg's eyes narrowed. Suspicion was growing like a weed.

"What are you talking about, Girl?"

"For starters, how did you become friends?"

Alan's sigh told Meg he was ready to confess. "Matt had a plan to bring you to Portland. He came to talk with your mother and me about it."

"Now I get the picture! And of course you just went along with it, not bothering to ask me how I felt about it!" Drat! The man was still meddling in her affairs!

"It wasn't like that, Meg. Matt has come to realize that it's important for you to make your own decisions. He was hoping that with a terrific job offer and a little more understanding from me, you might decide that Portland was where you wanted to be. I guess that was too much to hope for, but you've got to give him credit for trying.''

"He set the whole thing up? The interview? The talk you and I had? I hope he didn't arrange for your heart attack too!'' Meg's own heart, which had been softening towards Matt, suspended its thawing action.

"No, I'm responsible for that.'' Alan smiled a small, rueful smile. "Matt just shared what he'd come to understand about you. He thought I might benefit from his lesson. Of course, the whole plan fell through when you refused to have the interview. But the most important thing, to me at least, has been you and me coming to a better understanding. We can keep working on that, wherever you are.''

"Okay, so he gets credit for helping us get along better. I still don't like him trying to arrange my life, especially behind my back.''

"I believe you told him you didn't want to see him anymore?'' Alan's voice was gentle with amusement.

"Oh, that.''

"From what he said, you had good reason.''

"Are you trying to tell me that Matthew Aaberg actually understands why I was so angry with him? And if that's the case, why did he act like that in the first place?'' Meg asked, still skeptical.

"I believe he's gone through some kind of change. He said one of his sisters set him straight.''

"If that's really true, then . . .'' Meg's voice trailed off, her imagination igniting like wildfire. Could it be that he really had listened to her?

"Then it might be possible for you two to work something out?'' her father coached.

"I don't know, Dad . . .''

"Too risky?" Alan asked, echoing Matt's ploy with him.

Meg smiled fondly at her father. "You know us Careys, always ready to rise to the challenge. But it would help to know just why Matt wanted me to move back here. Did he say?" Meg held her breath, hoping against hope that her father had the answer she wanted to hear.

Alan reached for her hand. "He loves you, Meggie. He wants you to be happy."

Meg swallowed, trying to digest his words. "I've got to see him. Do you know how to get in touch with him?"

"I'm not sure he's back yet. He called a few days ago, just before I landed in here, and said it looked like he had a few more changes yet to make. He said that when he did that, he'd be back."

"What do you suppose he meant?" Would Matt always remain such a mystery to her?

"All I know is that he's done a lot of self-examination since you sent him away."

"So have I," she said.

"So have we all," Alan amended.

As soon as Meg got back to Hazel Creek, she tried calling Matt. True to her father's prediction, he didn't answer. She left a message on his machine. "Matt, this is Meg, please call me at my parents' house if you get back before Sunday. Thanks."

Chapter Nineteen

It had come to Matt like a rifle shot. He nearly dropped to his knees with its force. If he and Meg were going to be together, it was he who was going to have to make the supreme sacrifice. He would have to leave Portland, his job, his sisters, his friends, and start a new life in Los Angeles. Clearly it was the only way he could be with Meg.

Matt reflected on that moment of decision as he flew home to Oregon. He smiled a little wistfully to himself. He supposed he would always think of Oregon as home, no matter where he lived.

It appeared that his trip to L.A. had been successful. Matt expected more than one job offer in the next few weeks. Some of the work sounded interesting. One station talked about using him as a kind of environmental gadfly, combing the state of California for monthly exposés on ecological damage. Not quite what he might have chosen to do, but if he could be with Meg, he'd somehow manage the rest.

Still thinking about the changes that lay ahead of him, Matt almost missed the tall beauty going through the security check as he strode down the concourse. A flash of red hair caught his eye and he did a double take, then abruptly veered toward her, his heart hammering in his chest. "Meg!" he called, just as she stepped through the metal detector. She turned around on the other side of it and stared at him, wide-eyed, her mouth open in disbelief. He would remember that look as long as he lived. She stood suspended, caught between surprise and hope, fear and joy. Matt paused too, sensing that this was the moment that would mark the turning point of their lives. He reached his hand out to her from the opposite side of the machine. "Meg, please. I have to talk to you."

"I have to talk to you, too," she said. They continued to stand apart, neither one of them moving to the other side.

"Sir . . ." the security officer gestured to Matt. "Please go on through."

Regaining his senses, Matt dumped his briefcase and keys onto the conveyor belt and stepped towards Meg whose eyes never left him. His impulse was to put his arms around her and simply hold her for a long, long time, but the memory of their last time together restrained him. He steered her off to one side. "Meg, what are you doing here?"

Matt's touch, even through her coat, sent a thrill up her spine. She wanted to throw herself in his arms and tell him she loved him, but she was afraid of his response. Instead, she composed herself to answer his question. "Dad had a heart attack. He's going to be okay," she hurried to assure Matt when she saw the alarm in his face.

"Thank God! He was all right when I last talked with him. When did it happen?"

"Last Sunday afternoon."

"It must have been just after I left. Is he in the hospital? Can I see him?"

"He'll be coming home tomorrow sometime. I'm sure he would appreciate a call. He seems to think pretty highly of you. I can't imagine why."

Matt was so wrapped up in his guilt, he didn't see the twinkle in her eye. "Meg, I know you said you never wanted to see me again, but things have changed, I've changed. I . . ."

"I know, Matt," she interrupted. "I've changed too. I'd like to tell you about it."

"You've got a plane to catch."

"Yes." She paused, thinking she should go, knowing that she couldn't. "You know something, Matt? Some things are more important than planes . . . and jobs. How about that dinner you offered me in California? Those hot dogs hardly qualify. Is the offer still open?" Meg couldn't believe she was saying things that would have seemed heretical to her only a couple of weeks ago. But her heart was leading the way, and all she could do was hang on for dear life.

"Sure! Great!"

"Then let's go." Meg laughed, feeling deliciously liberated.

"What about your bags?" he asked, as they walked away from the gate.

"I just have one. I'll leave a message at the desk to have it picked up when it gets to L.A. Do you have some luggage to collect? Shall we meet back in the lobby?"

"Not on your life, Lady. You're not getting out of my sight." Matt tightened his grip on her arm.

"Is that a promise?" Meg demanded to know, stopping in mid stride and turning towards him.

He halted beside her, set his briefcase down, and put his

arms around her waist, pulling her so close that her breath caught in her throat. "I could demonstrate," he offered. Green eyes met golden-brown eyes.

"Mm. Maybe later," she teased, catching one of his hands in hers and breaking from his embrace. "So, where are we going for dinner?"

"How does Italian sound?"

"Italian's good." It could be Martian for all she cared.

Their mood changed as he drove toward the city. Matt, who had been so eager to share his news with her, couldn't seem to find the words to begin. Meg was having the same trouble. He stole frequent glances in her direction. She did the same with him. Once, their eyes met. They both looked quickly away. The air in the car hung heavy with unexpressed speculation. The enormity of the decision they both knew lay before them was sobering.

Finally reaching the restaurant, Matt escorted Meg inside where they were seated by the waiter. It was a typical small establishment, dark, with candles on the table that cast shadows on the plastic grapes and silk grape leaves intertwined on the latticed walls. They ordered, and then the waiter left them. Matt took a sip of the wine and cleared his throat just as Meg was about to speak. "I'm sorry, you go ahead," he said.

"No, you."

"Well, I was just going to tell you my news. I . . . well, I'm planning on moving to L.A., Meg. I've been down there interviewing this week, and I think I'll probably get a job offer. I was hoping that maybe we could, you know, see each other."

Meg's eyes grew wide with astonishment at his news. She fought the urge to smile, to laugh, to jump for joy. "I'm sorry, Matt," she said as seriously as she could manage, shaking her head slightly. "I don't think that will work out at all."

"You won't give me another chance?"

"I think you ought to stick to your original plan," she said, allowing a smile to touch her lips.

"My plan? It stinks!"

"Maybe you need to have a little more faith in it, and in me, Matt."

"But you love L.A. Besides, Rosalind took the job . . ."

"I'll tell you about that later. It seems that homing device of yours . . . ours . . . works both ways and can't easily be removed. The fact that we found each other at the airport tonight proves it."

"I still don't see . . ."

"It just so happens that there are at least two important reasons I have for moving here."

"For moving here?" Matt echoed. His heart beat a little faster.

"My parents, for one. Dad and I have finally been able to talk. This week has been a real blessing, and I know you had a hand in it. The second," she went on before he could respond, "is you. I don't want to take the chance of losing you again." She smiled and stretched her hands across the table.

"Do you mean that, Meg?" He grasped her hands like a thirsty man reaching for a cold glass of water. "Meggie," he said softly, "I love you. Will you marry me?" The words he had been longing to say poured out, strong and sure.

"Yes, Matthew, I love you too, and I want to be with you. Always."

Before further words could be uttered, the waiter brought their food and placed it in front of them. He refilled their wineglasses, then left. Meg picked up her fork and twirled the spaghetti around it. Abruptly, she put it back down, leaned across the table and said confidentially to Matt, "I'm not the least bit hungry."

A grin creased Matt's face. "Neither am I. Would you like to go for a walk?"

Meg nodded.

It took some convincing for the waiter to understand that they wanted the check, and that no, there was nothing wrong with the food or the service. Meg was convulsed with giggles by the time they were able to make an exit. They stood together on the sidewalk for several moments, hugging and kissing and laughing. A light spring rain had begun to fall, but they took no notice.

Meg gave her mother no explanation for her return to home that evening, nor for her missing luggage. She hurried off to bed before the confused Pam had a chance to question her. Meg was glad she would not have to keep her secret long.

The next day, Pam and Meg drove together to the hospital to bring Alan home. There, more surprises awaited. Matt, who had been impatiently pacing the hospital lobby, greeted Pam warmly. Then, with a big smile, he put his arm around Meg and gave her a kiss which lasted several moments.

"Did I miss something?" Pam asked, clearly pleased.

Meg released herself from Matt's embrace and laughed, radiating happiness.

"Don't tell me. I know that look. Have you set a date?"

"Mother!"

"I hope you'll have the wedding at our home. We can put off selling the house for a little while. It would be nice having it in the garden when the weather gets warmer. Eliza Jane will be the flower girl, of course."

Meg looked over at Matt wondering what his reaction would be. He ran his fingers through his hair, then turned and loudly whispered in Meg's ear. "What say we get married today? We can drop by the courthouse on the way to your folks' house. I know a justice of the peace who . . ."

Pam laughed. "All right, Matt, you called my bluff. It's up to you two, of course. I'm just delighted that you've both finally come to your senses." She gave each of her "children" a buzz on the cheek and hurried off to sign Alan's release forms.

Matt turned to Meg. What's this about your folks selling their house?" he asked. Tears sprang to Meg's eyes. She'd known about it for the last day, but had been too busy to let it sink in.

"I'm sorry," Matt said softly, drawing Meg into his arms. His sympathy released more tears, and he petted and rocked her as she grieved for the loss of her childhood home. When she had quieted, he spoke. "We'll make our own home, Meggie," he said, brushing away her tears. "A home where we and our loved ones will always be welcome. A home of our hearts."

Meg began adding more of Matt's attributes to her list: *loving, tender, passionate* . . . The thought came to her that although the list now seemed complete, she had a lifetime for additions.